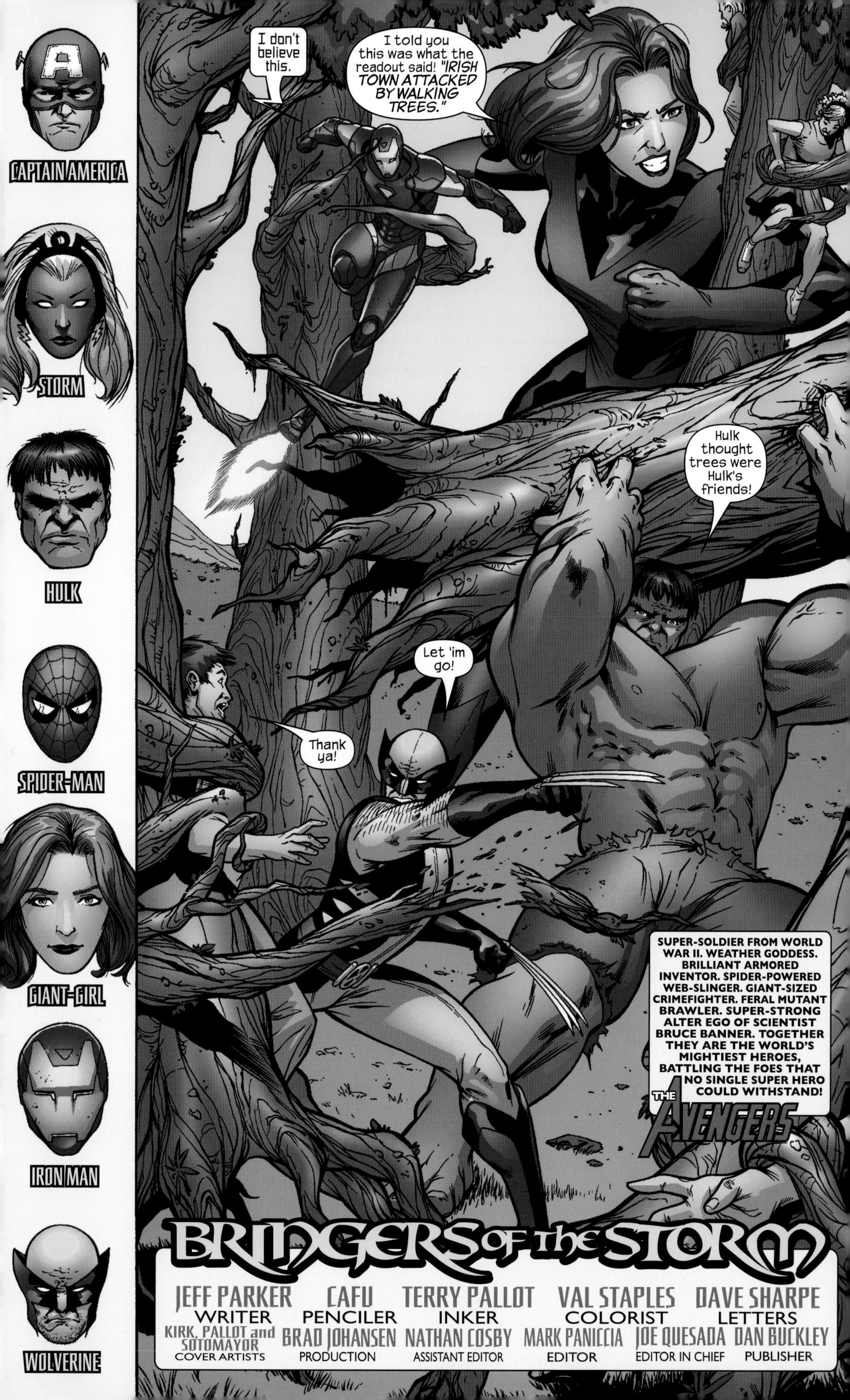
CAPTAIN AMERICA
STORM
HULK
SPIDER-MAN
GIANT-GIRL
IRON MAN
WOLVERINE
I don't believe this.
I told you this was what the readout said! "IRISH TOWN ATTACKED BY WALKING TREES."
Hulk thought trees were Hulk's friends!
Let 'im go!
Thank ya!
SUPER-SOLDIER FROM WORLD WAR II. WEATHER GODDESS. BRILLIANT ARMORED INVENTOR. SPIDER-POWERED WEB-SLINGER. GIANT-SIZED CRIMEFIGHTER. FERAL MUTANT BRAWLER. SUPER-STRONG ALTER EGO OF SCIENTIST BRUCE BANNER. TOGETHER THEY ARE THE WORLD'S MIGHTIEST HEROES, BATTLING THE FOES THAT NO SINGLE SUPER HERO COULD WITHSTAND!
THE AVENGERS
BRINGERS OF THE STORM
JEFF PARKER WRITER
CAFU PENCILER
TERRY PALLOT INKER
VAL STAPLES COLORIST
DAVE SHARPE LETTERS
KIRK, PALLOT and SOTOMAYOR COVER ARTISTS
BRAD JOHANSEN PRODUCTION
NATHAN COSBY ASSISTANT EDITOR
MARK PANICCIA EDITOR
JOE QUESADA EDITOR IN CHIEF
DAN BUCKLEY PUBLISHER

WWW.ABDOPUBLISHING.COM

Reinforced library bound edition published in 2015 by Spotlight,
a division of ABDO, PO Box 398166, Minneapolis, Minnesota 55439.
Spotlight produces high-quality reinforced library bound editions for
schools and libraries. Published by agreement with Marvel Characters, Inc.

Printed in the United States of America, North Mankato, Minnesota.
052014
072014

THIS BOOK CONTAINS
RECYCLED MATERIALS

Marvel.com
© 2015 Marvel

LIBRARY OF CONGRESS CATALOGING-IN-PUBLICATION DATA

Parker, Jeff, 1966-
  The Avengers. set 4 / Jeff Parker, writer ; Leonard Park, penciler ; Terry
Pallot, inker ; Val Staples, colorist ; Dave Sharpe, letters ; Kirk, Pallot, and
Sotomayer, cover artists. -- Reinforced library bound edition.
    pages cm
  ISBN 978-1-61479-293-2 (Attack of the 50 foot girl!) -- ISBN 978-1-61479-
294-9 (The avenging seven) -- ISBN 978-1-61479-295-6 (Bringers of the
Storm) -- ISBN 978-1-61479-296-3 (Even a Hawkeye can cry!)
1. Graphic novels. I. Kirk, Leonard, illustrator. II. Pallot, Terry, illustrator. III.
Sotomayor, Chris, illustrator. IV. Avengers (Comic strip) V. Title.
  PZ7.7.P252Ave 2015
  741.5'973--dc23

                                        2014005384

Spotlight

A Division of ABDO
www.abdopublishing.com

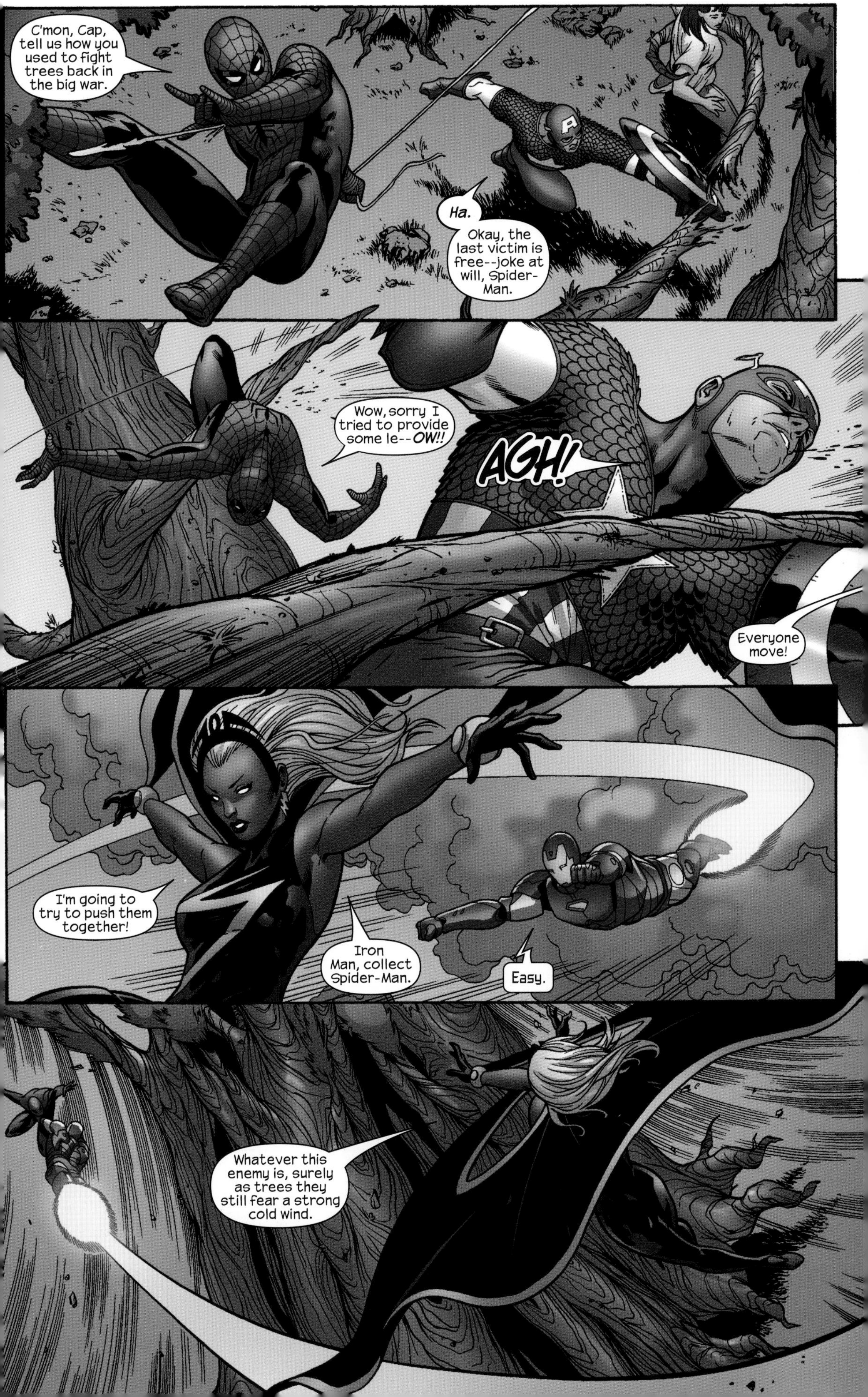
C'mon, Cap, tell us how you used to fight trees back in the big war.
Ha.
Okay, the last victim is free--joke at will, Spider-Man.
Wow, sorry I tried to provide some le--OW!!
AGH!
Everyone move!
I'm going to try to push them together!
Iron Man, collect Spider-Man.
Easy.
Whatever this enemy is, surely as trees they still fear a strong cold wind.

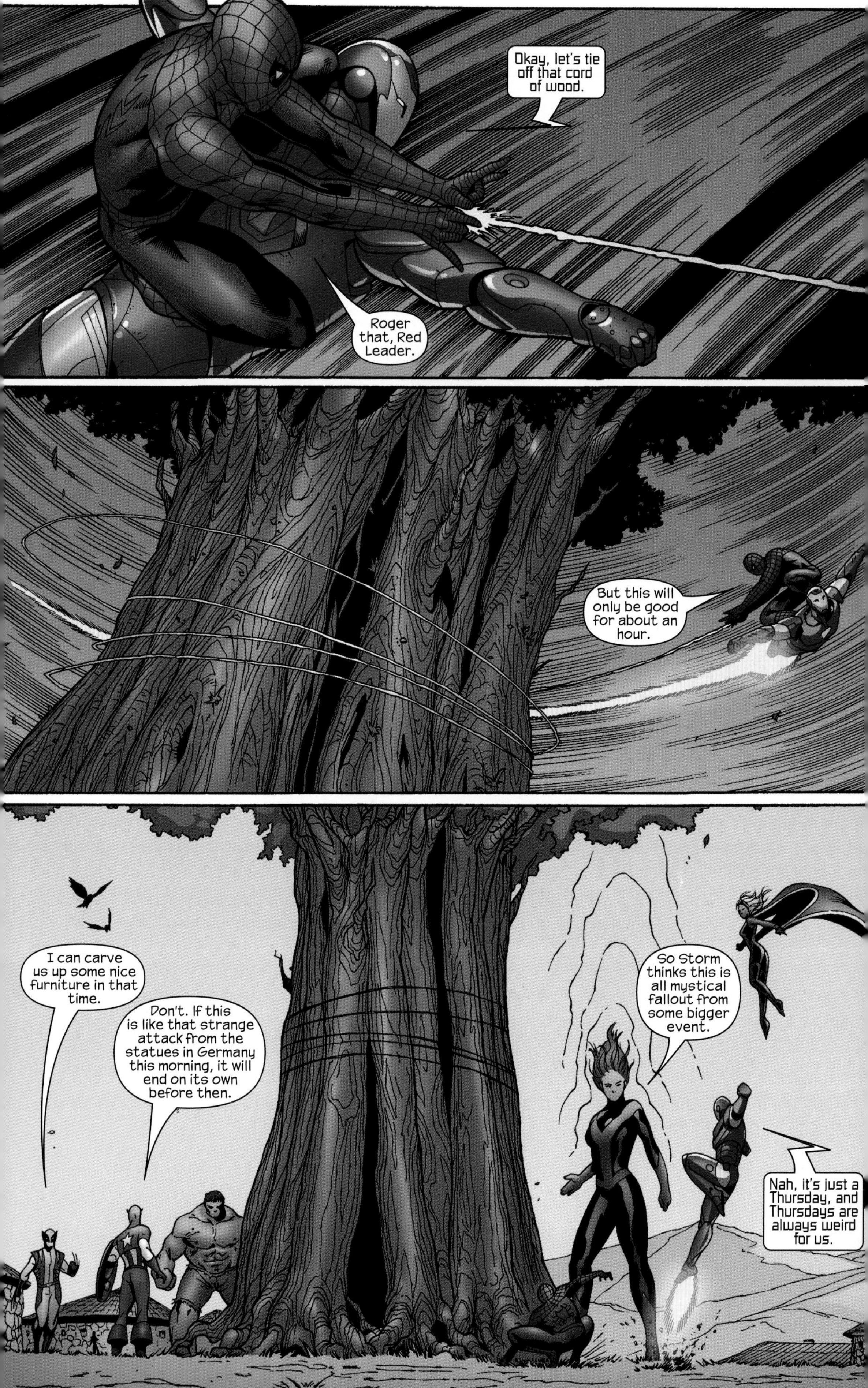

Okay, let's tie off that cord of wood.
Roger that, Red Leader.
But this will only be good for about an hour.
I can carve us up some nice furniture in that time.
Don't. If this is like that strange attack from the statues in Germany this morning, it will end on its own before then.
So Storm thinks this is all mystical fallout from some bigger event.
Nah, it's just a Thursday, and Thursdays are always weird for us.

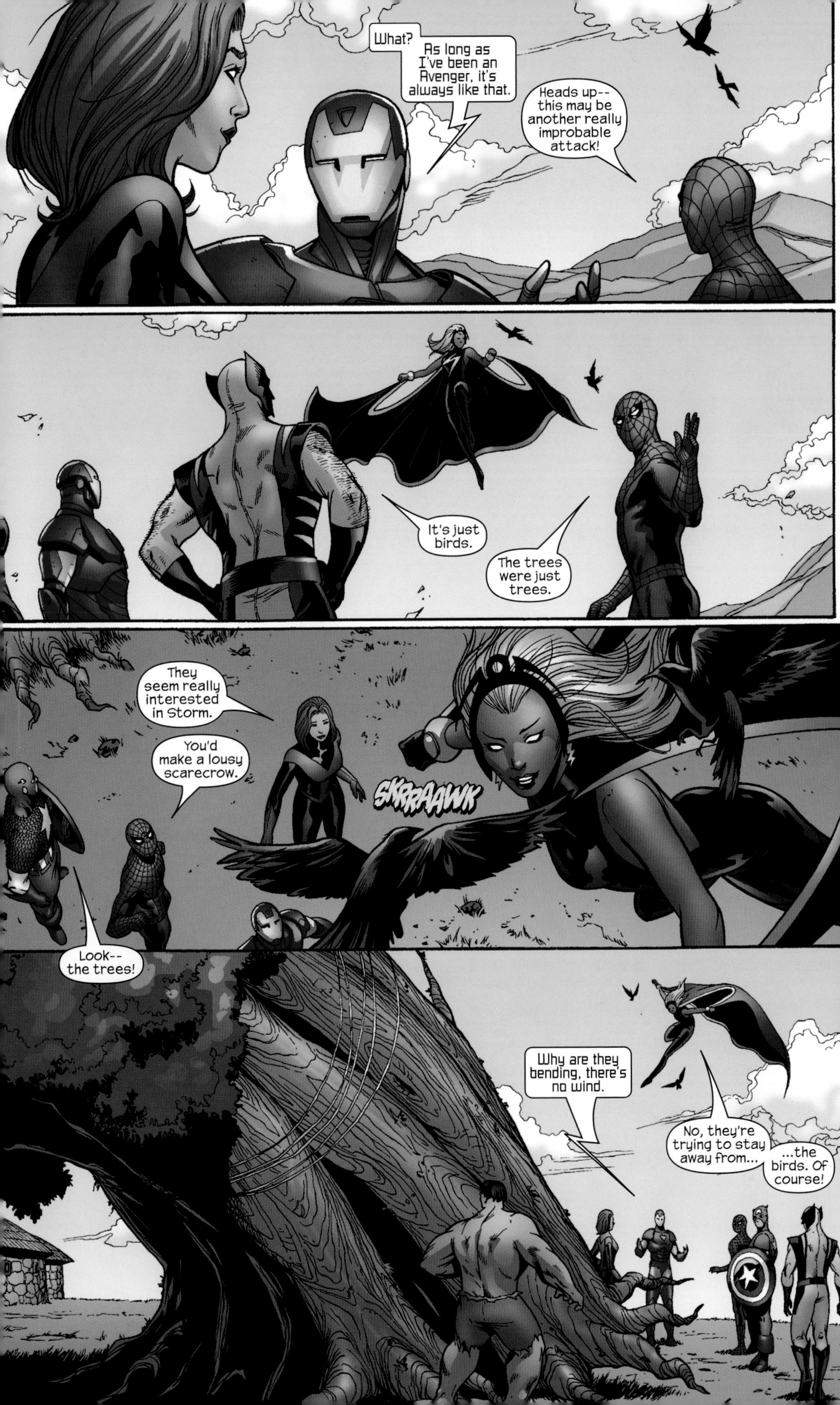
What?
As long as I've been an Avenger, it's always like that.
Heads up-- this may be another really improbable attack!
It's just birds.
The trees were just trees.
They seem really interested in Storm.
You'd make a lousy scarecrow.
SKRRAAWK
Look-- the trees!
Why are they bending, there's no wind.
No, they're trying to stay away from...
...the birds. Of course!

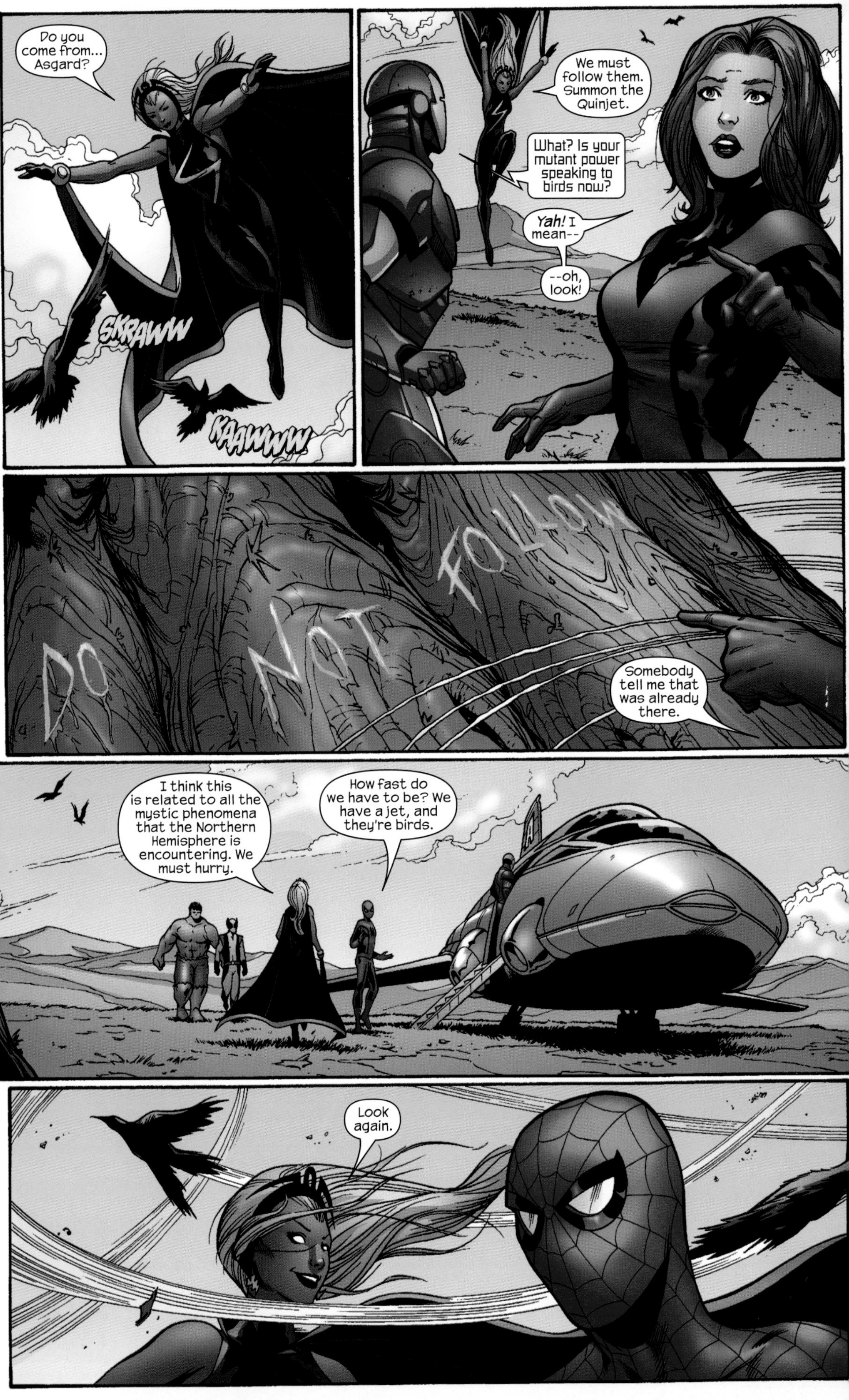
Do you come from... Asgard?
SKRAWW
KAAWWW
We must follow them. Summon the Quinjet.
What? Is your mutant power speaking to birds now?
Yah! I mean--
--oh, look!
DO NOT FOLLOW
Somebody tell me that was already there.
I think this is related to all the mystic phenomena that the Northern Hemisphere is encountering. We must hurry.
How fast do we have to be? We have a jet, and they're birds.
Look again.

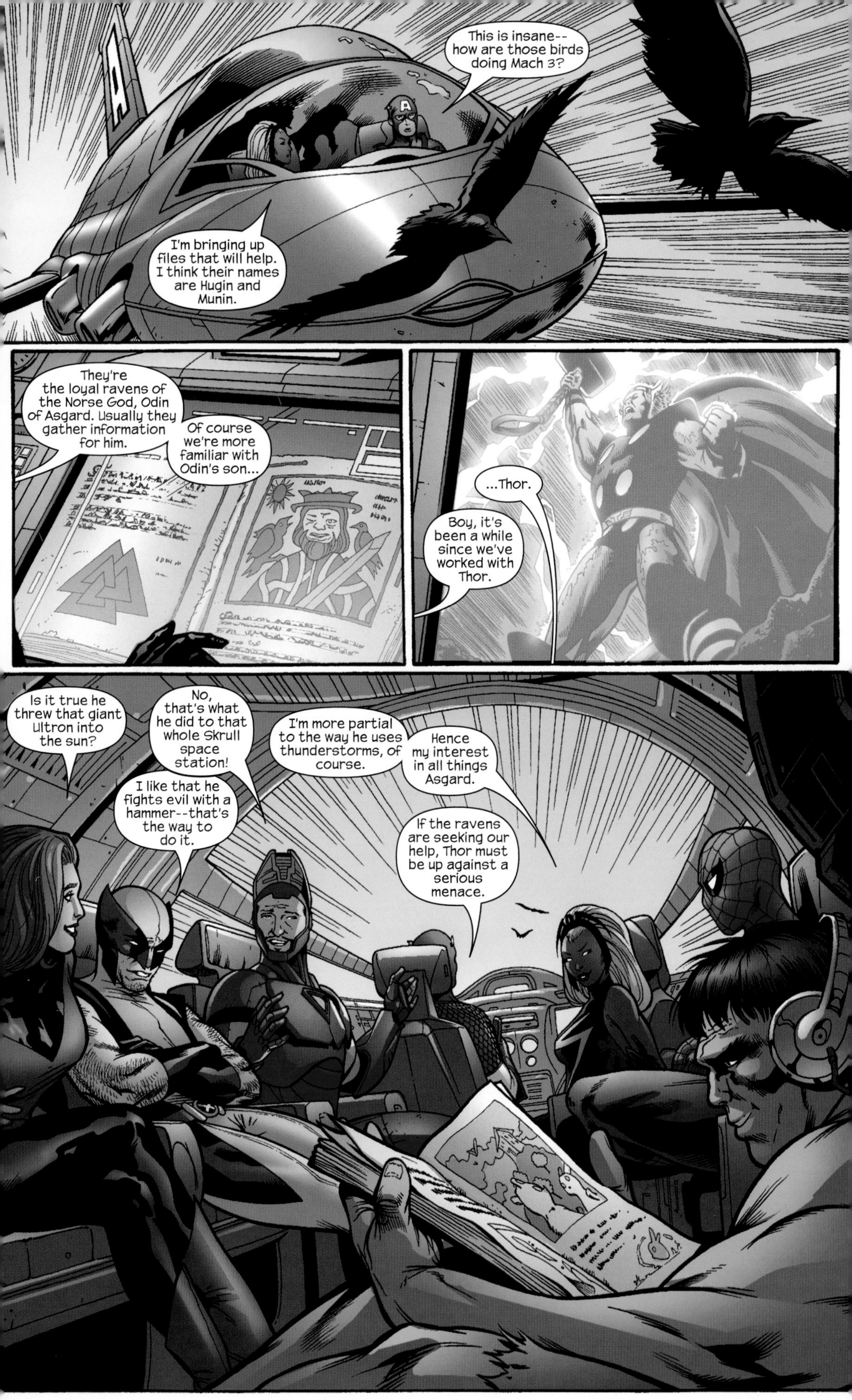
This is insane--how are those birds doing Mach 3?
I'm bringing up files that will help. I think their names are Hugin and Munin.
They're the loyal ravens of the Norse God, Odin of Asgard. Usually they gather information for him.
Of course we're more familiar with Odin's son...
...Thor.
Boy, it's been a while since we've worked with Thor.
Is it true he threw that giant Ultron into the sun?
No, that's what he did to that whole Skrull space station!
I like that he fights evil with a hammer--that's the way to do it.
I'm more partial to the way he uses thunderstorms, of course.
Hence my interest in all things Asgard.
If the ravens are seeking our help, Thor must be up against a serious menace.

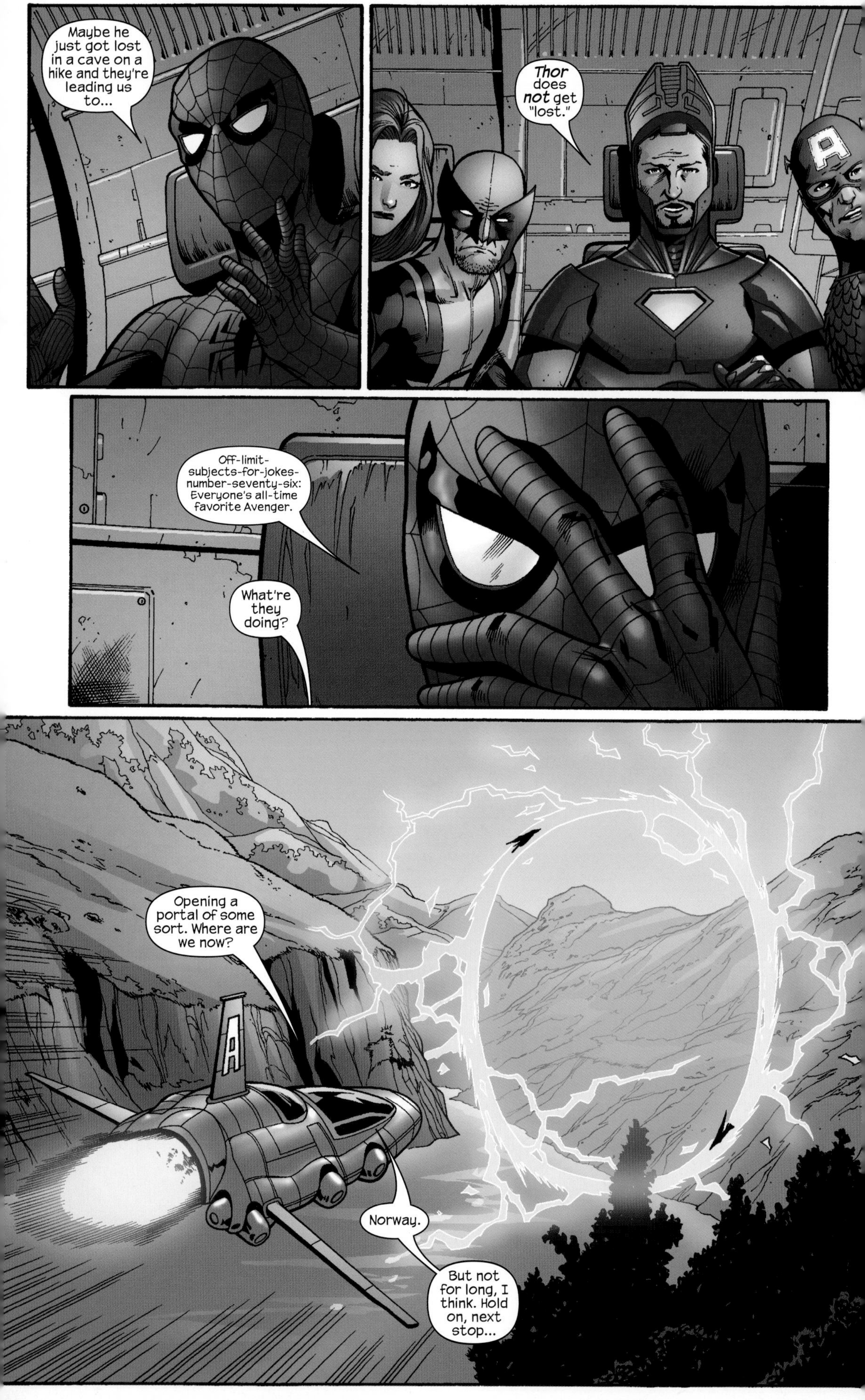
Maybe he just got lost in a cave on a hike and they're leading us to...
Thor does not get "lost."
Off-limit-subjects-for-jokes-number-seventy-six: Everyone's all-time favorite Avenger.
What're they doing?
Opening a portal of some sort. Where are we now?
Norway.
But not for long, I think. Hold on, next stop...

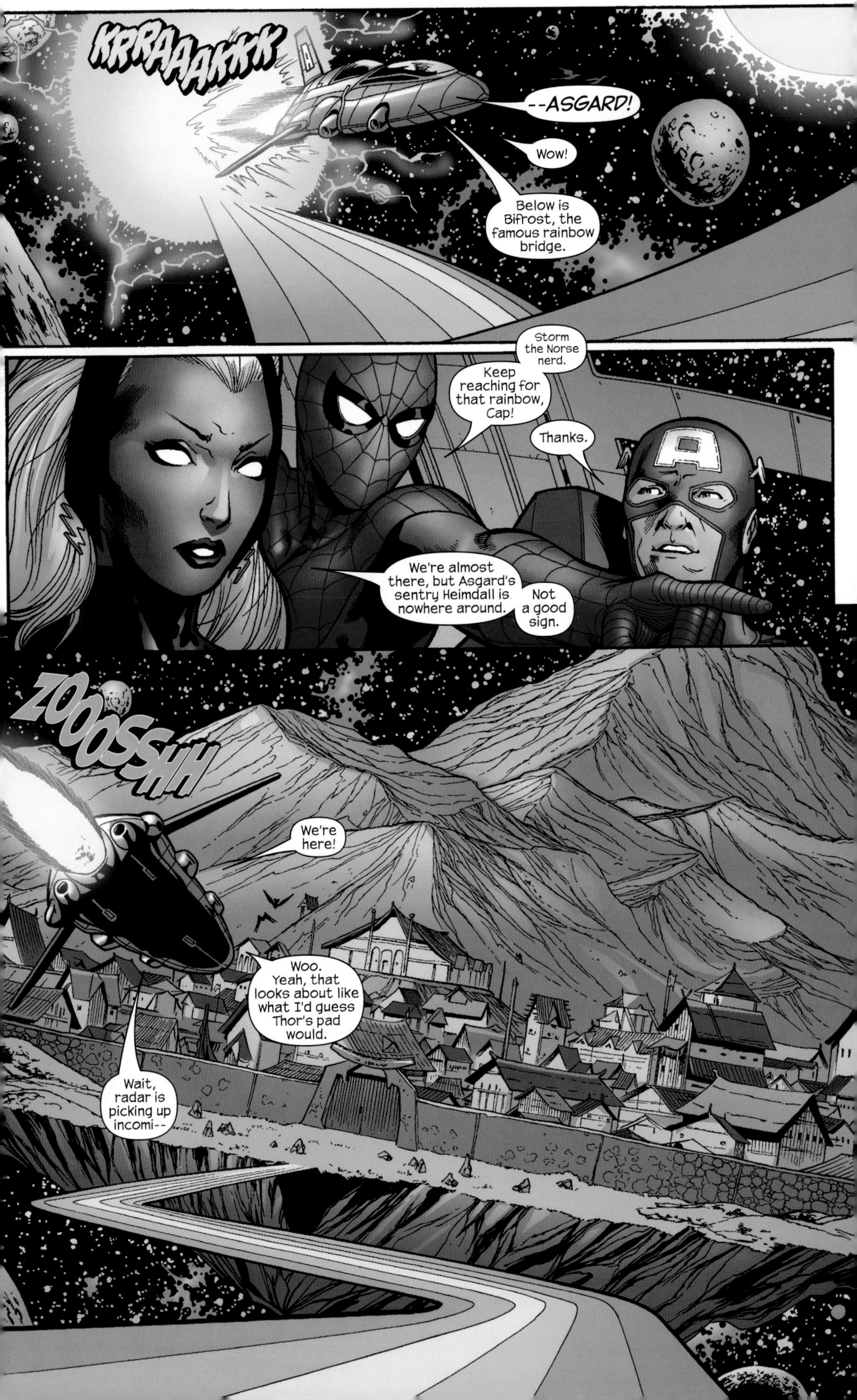
KRRAAAKKK
--ASGARD!
Wow!
Below is Bifrost, the famous rainbow bridge.
Storm the Norse nerd.
Keep reaching for that rainbow, Cap!
Thanks.
We're almost there, but Asgard's sentry Heimdall is nowhere around.
Not a good sign.
ZOOOSSHH
We're here!
Woo. Yeah, that looks about like what I'd guess Thor's pad would.
Wait, radar is picking up incomi--

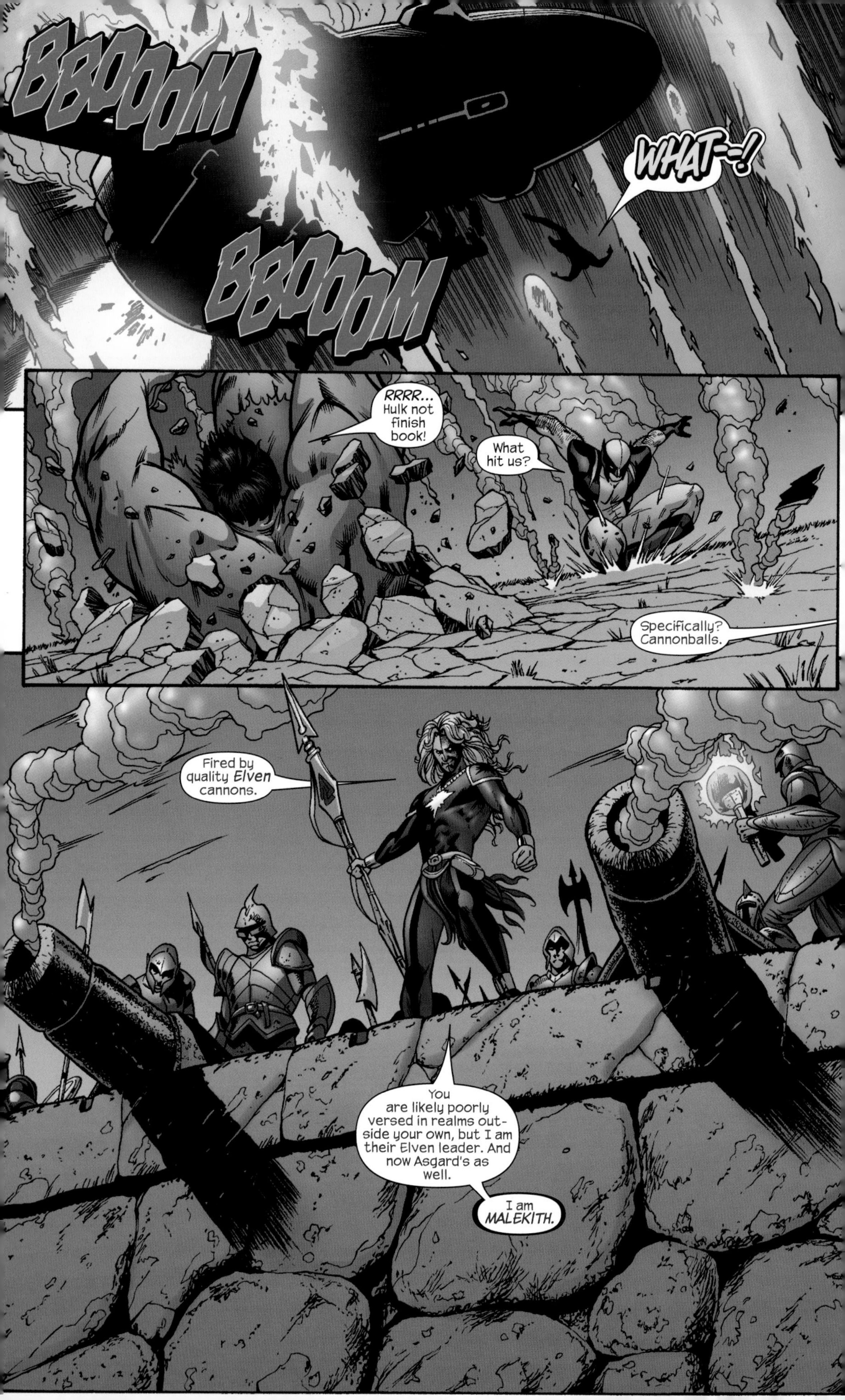
BBOOOOM
WHAT--!
BBOOOOM
RRRR... Hulk not finish book!
What hit us?
Specifically? Cannonballs.
Fired by quality Elven cannons.
You are likely poorly versed in realms outside your own, but I am their Elven leader. And now Asgard's as well.
I am MALEKITH.

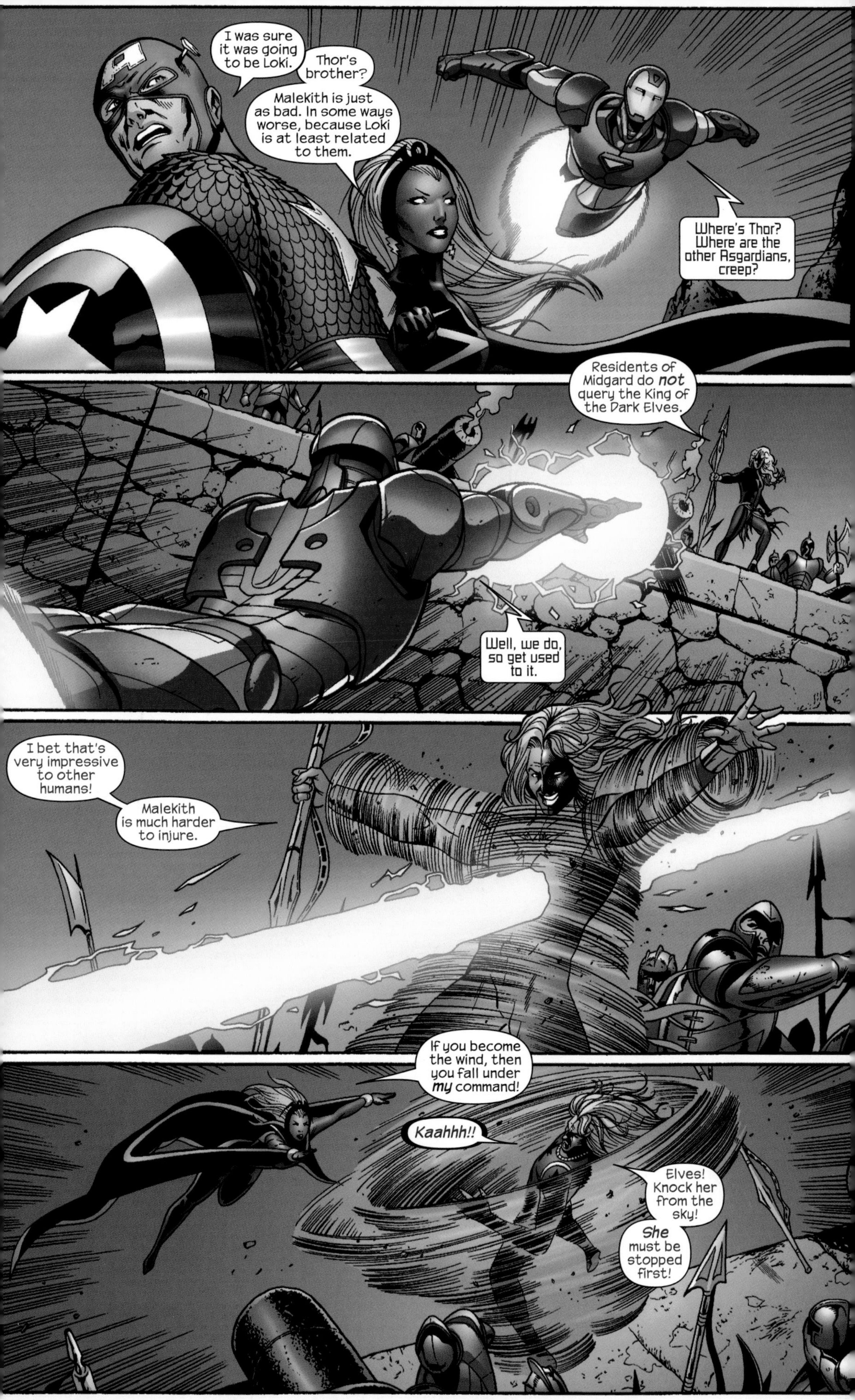

I was sure it was going to be Loki.
Thor's brother?
Malekith is just as bad. In some ways worse, because Loki is at least related to them.
Where's Thor? Where are the other Asgardians, creep?
Residents of Midgard do *not* query the King of the Dark Elves.
Well, we do, so get used to it.
I bet that's very impressive to other humans!
Malekith is much harder to injure.
If you become the wind, then you fall under *my* command!
Kaahhh!!
Elves! Knock her from the sky!
She must be stopped first!

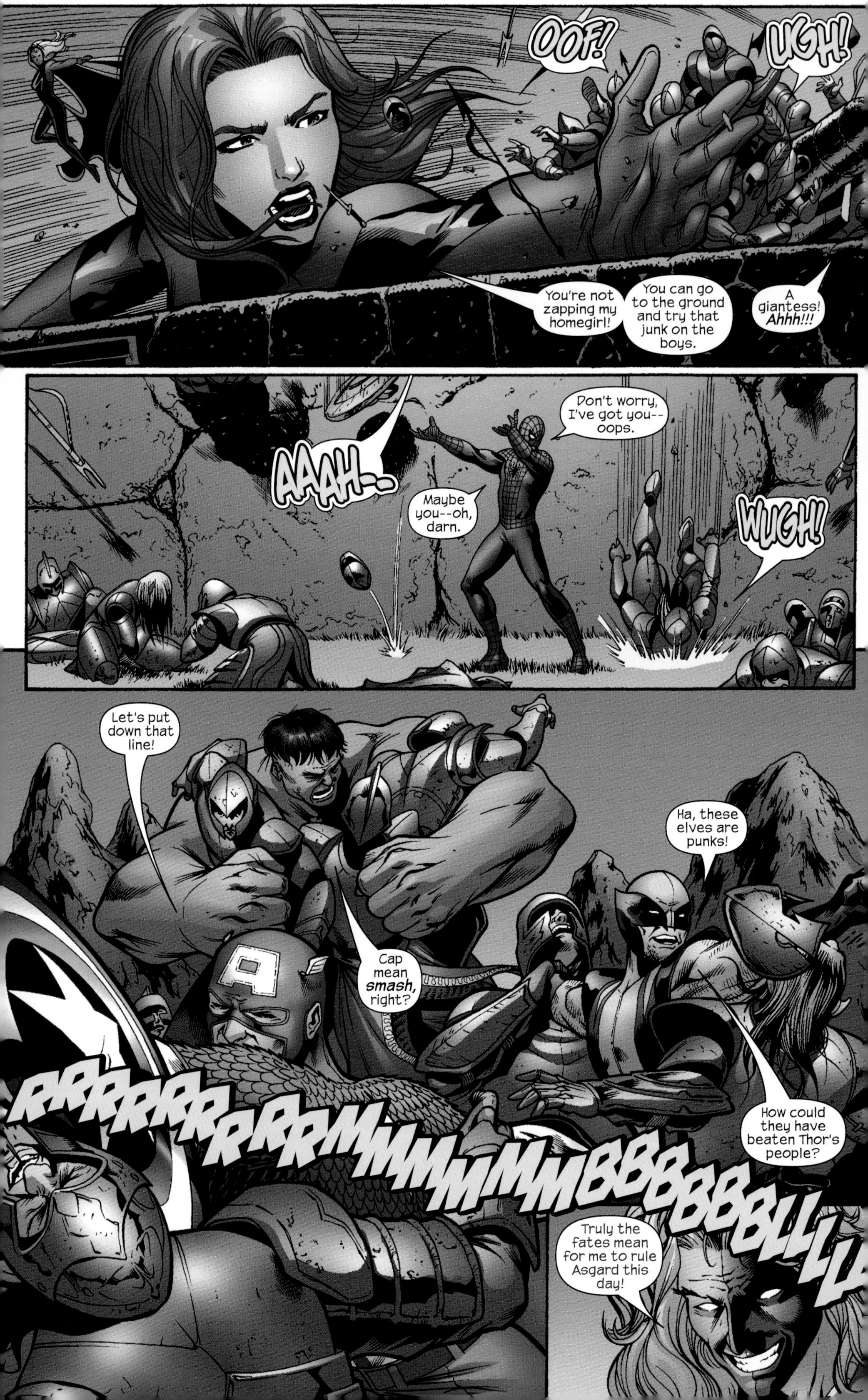
OOF!
UGH!
You're not zapping my homegirl!
You can go to the ground and try that junk on the boys.
A giantess! *Ahhh!!!*
Don't worry, I've got you-- oops.
AAAH--
Maybe you--oh, darn.
WUGH!
Let's put down that line!
Ha, these elves are punks!
Cap mean *smash,* right?
How could they have beaten Thor's people?
RRRRRRRRRMMMMMMMMBBBBBBBLLLL
Truly the fates mean for me to rule Asgard this day!

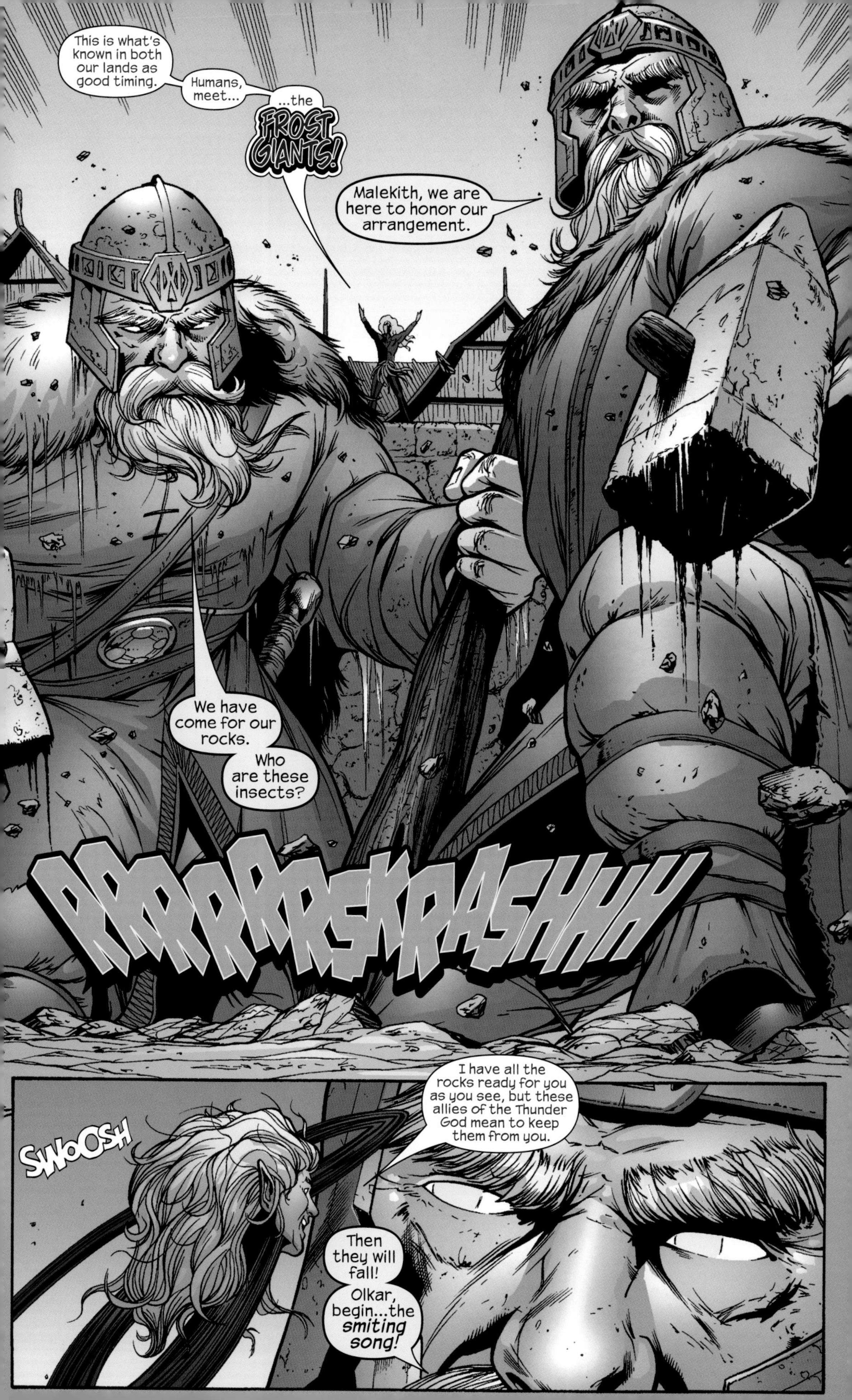
This is what's known in both our lands as good timing.
Humans, meet...
...the
FROST GIANTS!
Malekith, we are here to honor our arrangement.
We have come for our rocks.
Who are these insects?
RRRRRRSKRASHHH
SWOOSH
I have all the rocks ready for you as you see, but these allies of the Thunder God mean to keep them from you.
Then they will fall!
Olkar, begin...the *smiting song!*

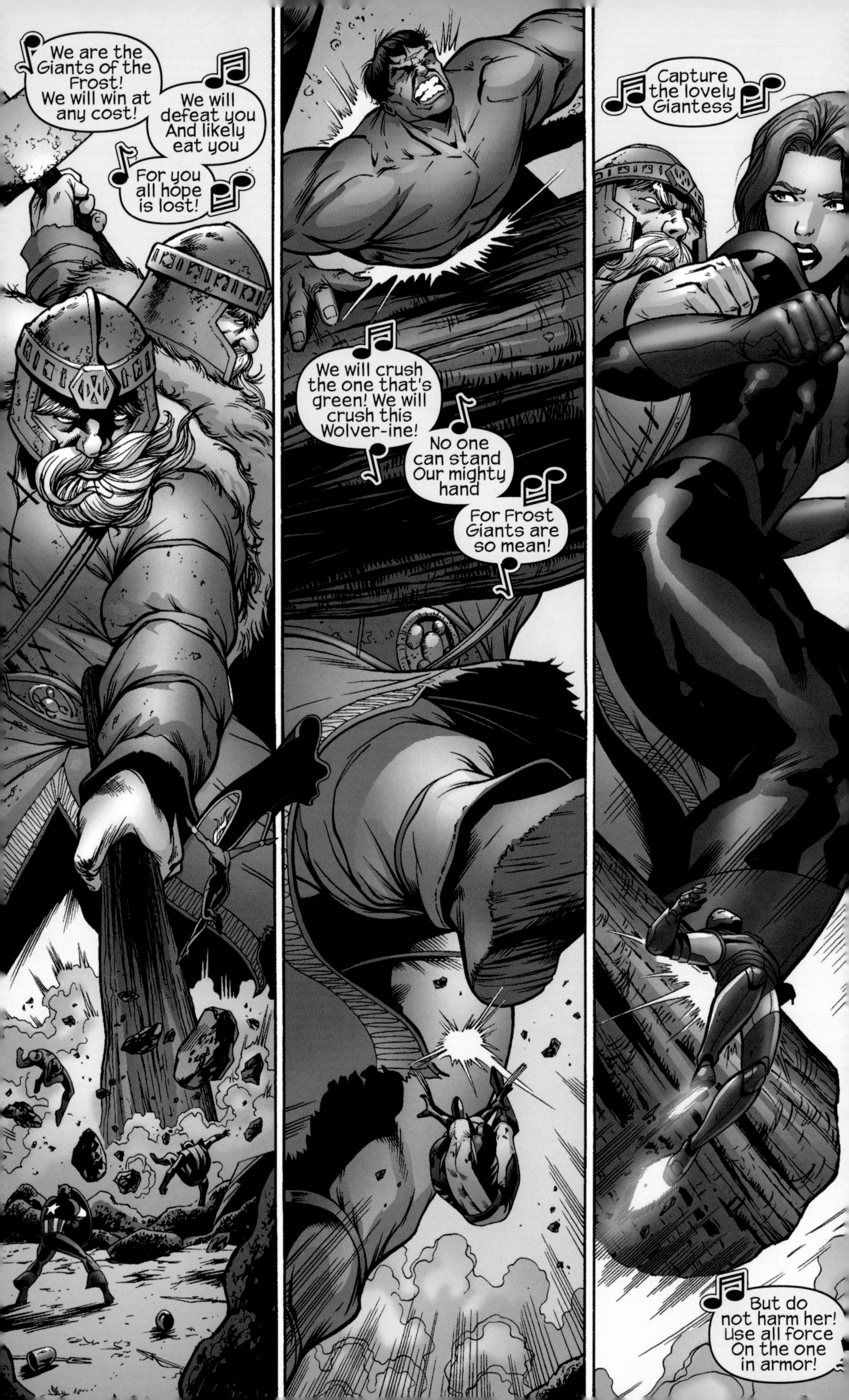
We are the Giants of the Frost! We will win at any cost!
We will defeat you And likely eat you
For you all hope is lost!
We will crush the one that's green! We will crush this Wolver-ine!
No one can stand Our mighty hand
For Frost Giants are so mean!
Capture the lovely Giantess
But do not harm her! Use all force On the one in armor!

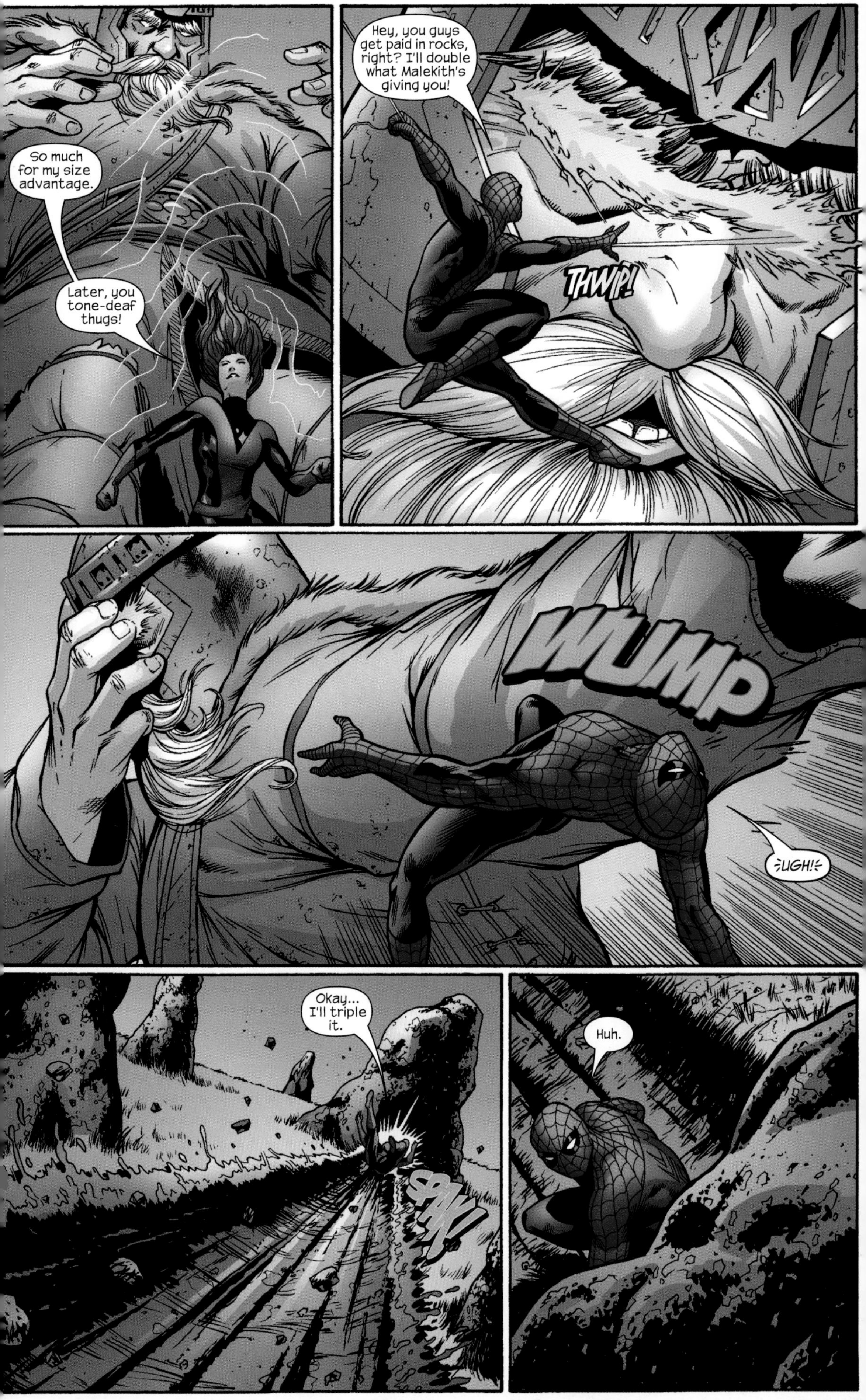
So much for my size advantage.
Later, you tone-deaf thugs!
Hey, you guys get paid in rocks, right? I'll double what Malekith's giving you!
THWIP!
WUMP
UGH!
Okay... I'll triple it.
SPAK!
Huh.

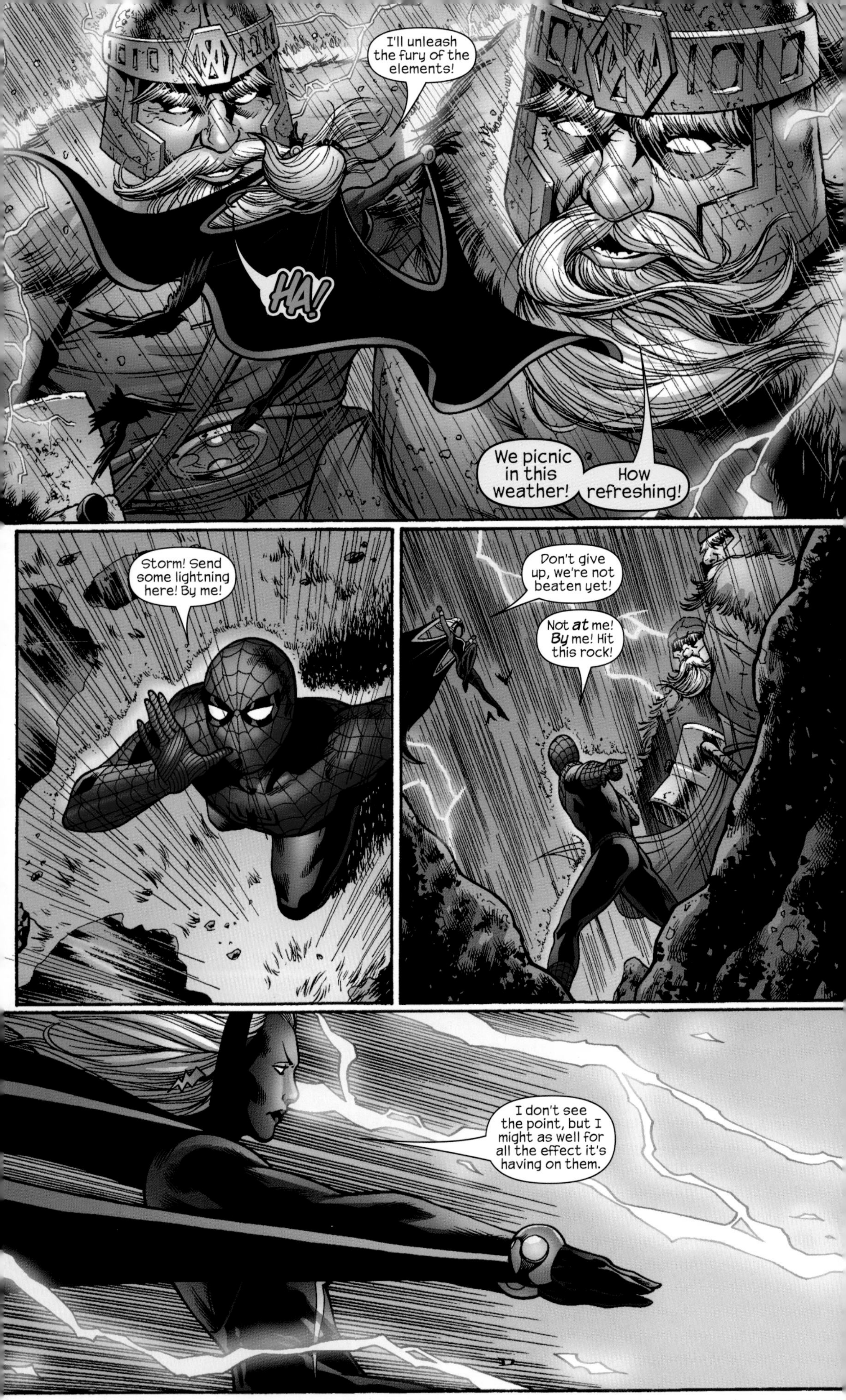
I'll unleash the fury of the elements!
HA!
We picnic in this weather!
How refreshing!
Storm! Send some lightning here! By me!
Don't give up, we're not beaten yet!
Not at me! By me! Hit this rock!
I don't see the point, but I might as well for all the effect it's having on them.

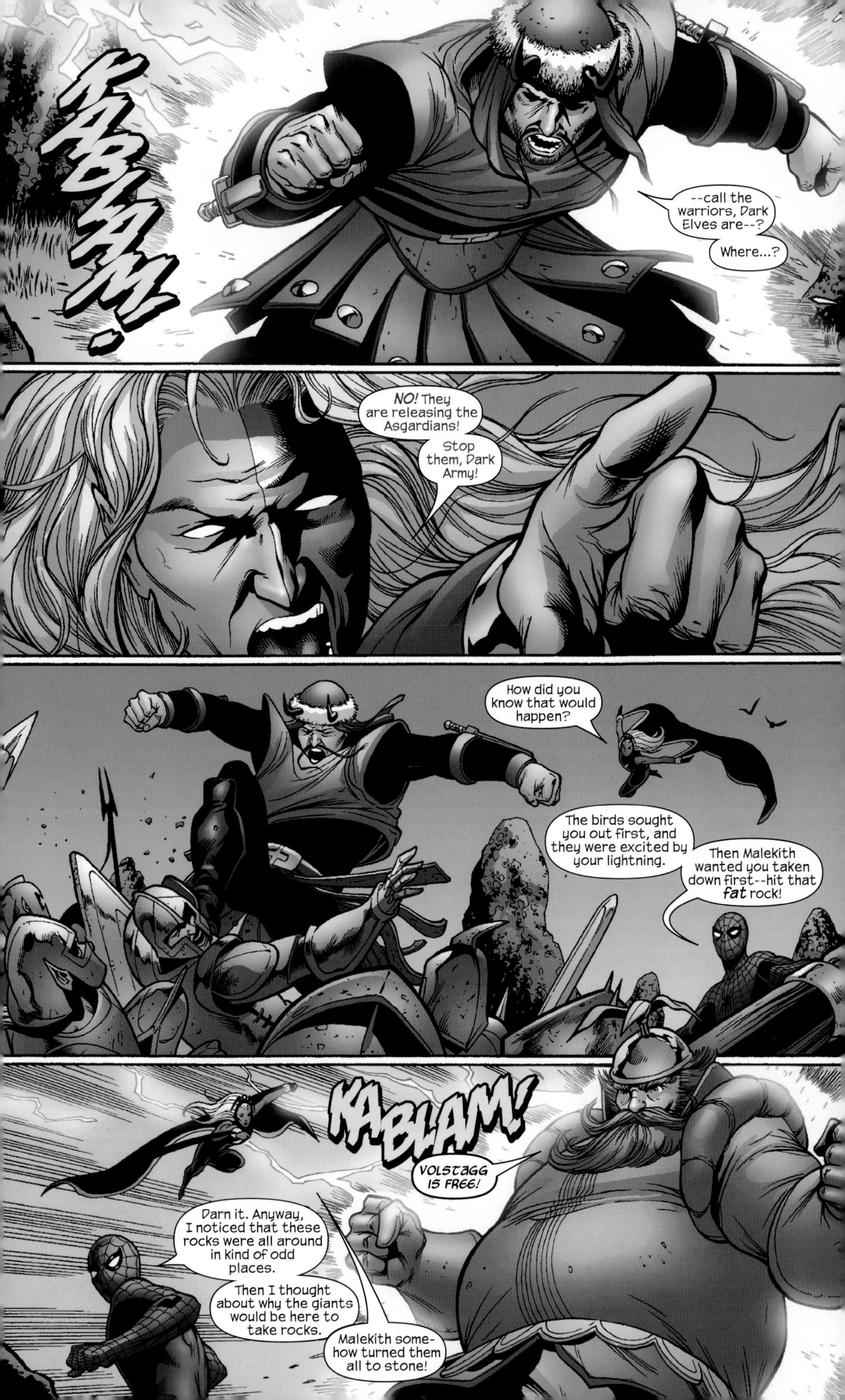
KABLAM!
--call the warriors, Dark Elves are--?
Where...?
NO! They are releasing the Asgardians!
Stop them, Dark Army!
How did you know that would happen?
The birds sought you out first, and they were excited by your lightning.
Then Malekith wanted you taken down first--hit that fat rock!
KABLAM!
VOLSTAGG IS FREE!
Darn it. Anyway, I noticed that these rocks were all around in kind of odd places.
Then I thought about why the giants would be here to take rocks.
Malekith some-how turned them all to stone!

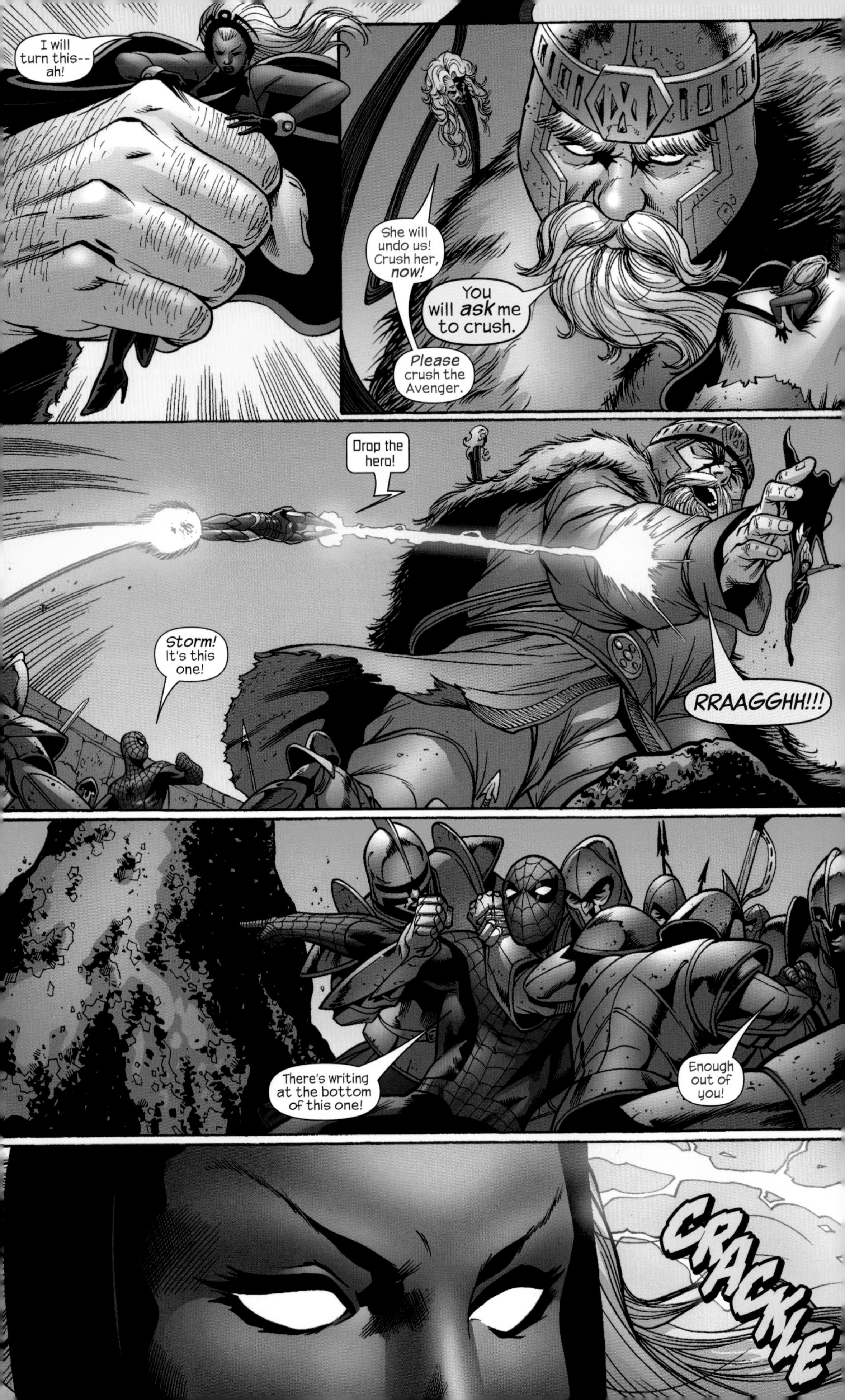

I will turn this-- ah!
She will undo us! Crush her, *now!*
You will **ask** me to crush.
Please crush the Avenger.
Drop the hero!
Storm! It's this one!
RRAAGGHH!!!
There's writing at the bottom of this one!
Enough out of you!
CRACKLE

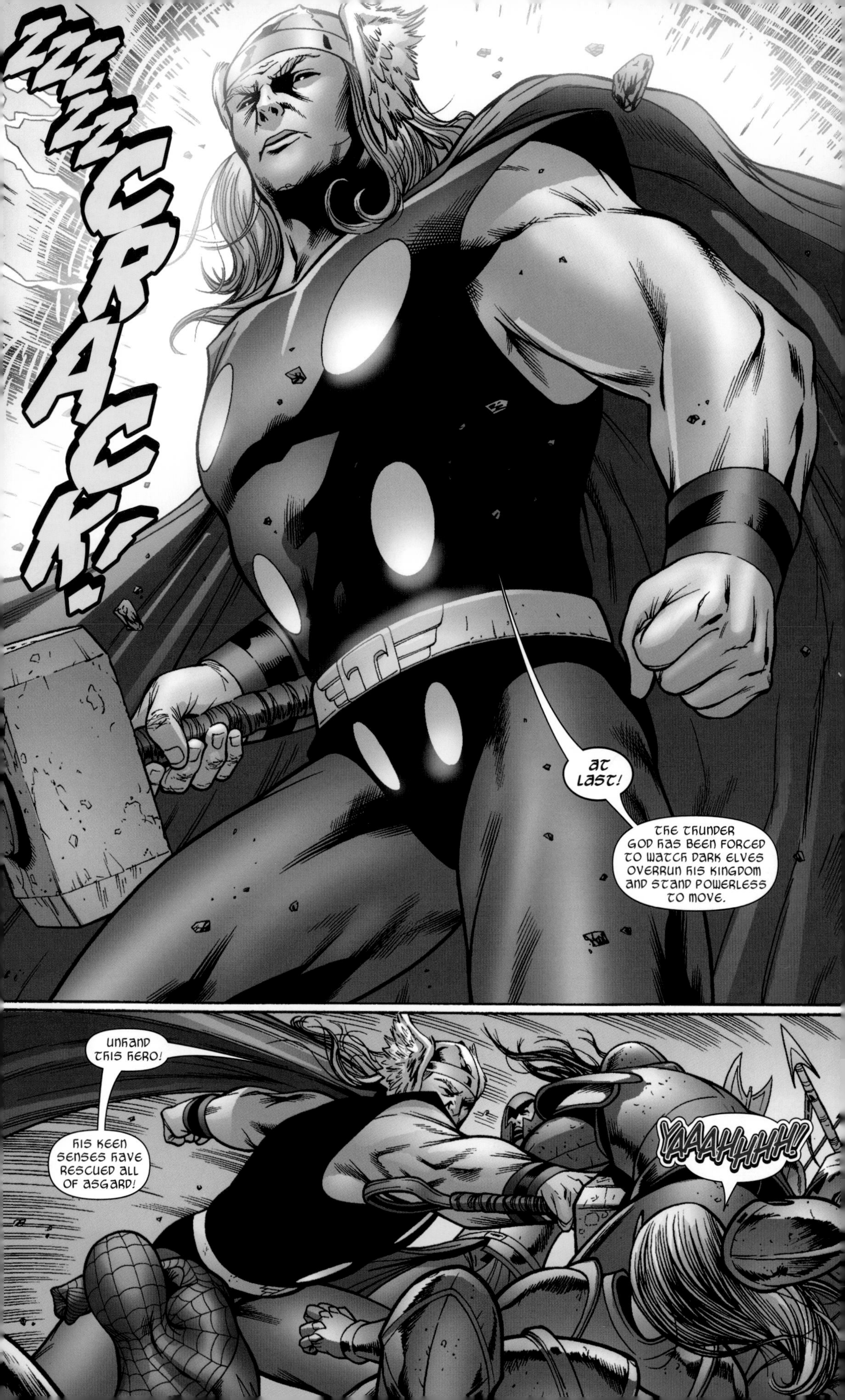
ZZZZZZCRACK!
AT LAST!
THE THUNDER GOD HAS BEEN FORCED TO WATCH DARK ELVES OVERRUN HIS KINGDOM AND STAND POWERLESS TO MOVE.
UNHAND THIS HERO!
HIS KEEN SENSES HAVE RESCUED ALL OF ASGARD!
YAAAHHHH!

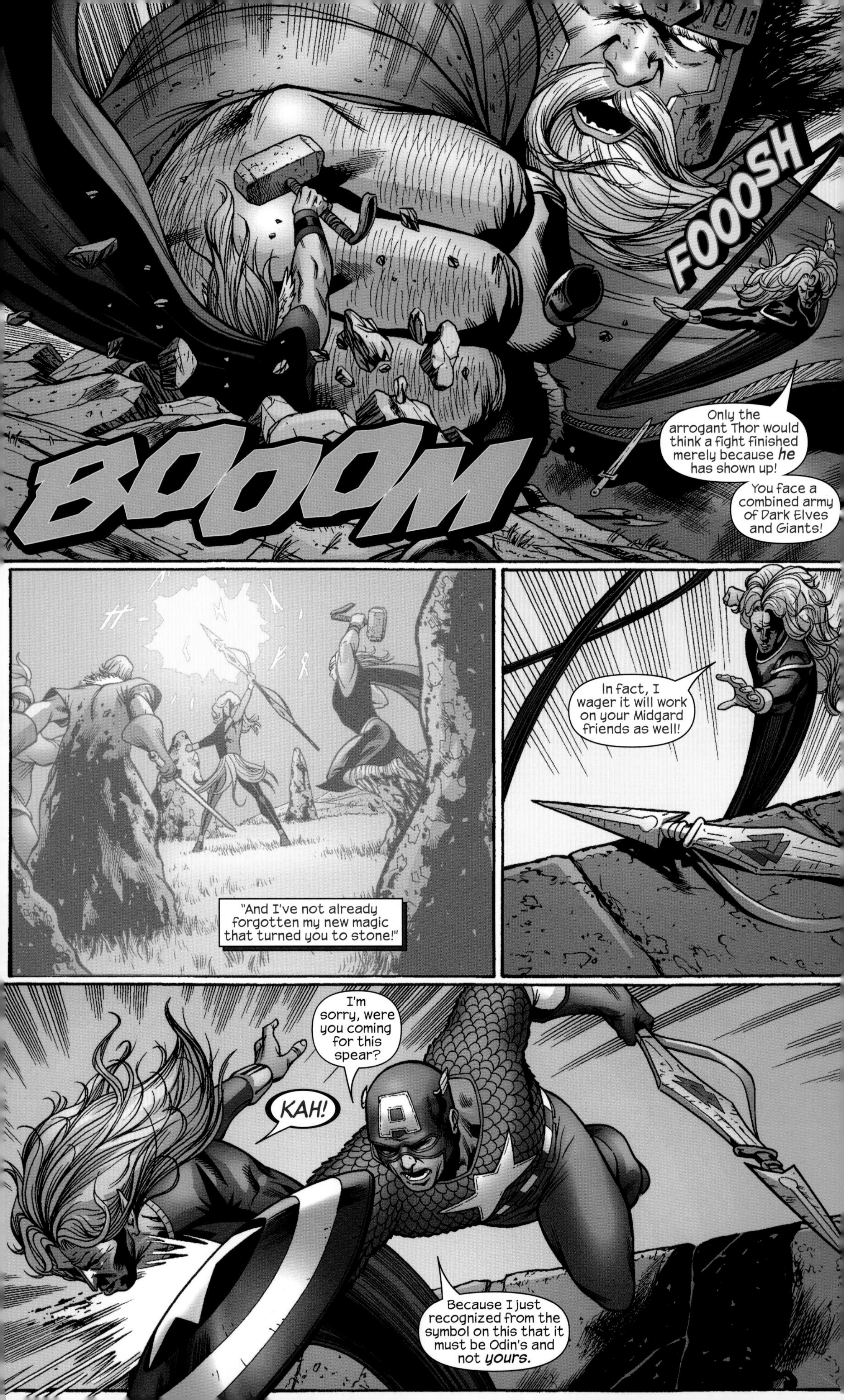
BOOOM
FOOOSH
Only the arrogant Thor would think a fight finished merely because *he* has shown up!
You face a combined army of Dark Elves and Giants!
"And I've not already forgotten my new magic that turned you to stone!"
In fact, I wager it will work on your Midgard friends as well!
I'm sorry, were you coming for this spear?
KAH!
Because I just recognized from the symbol on this that it must be Odin's and not *yours.*

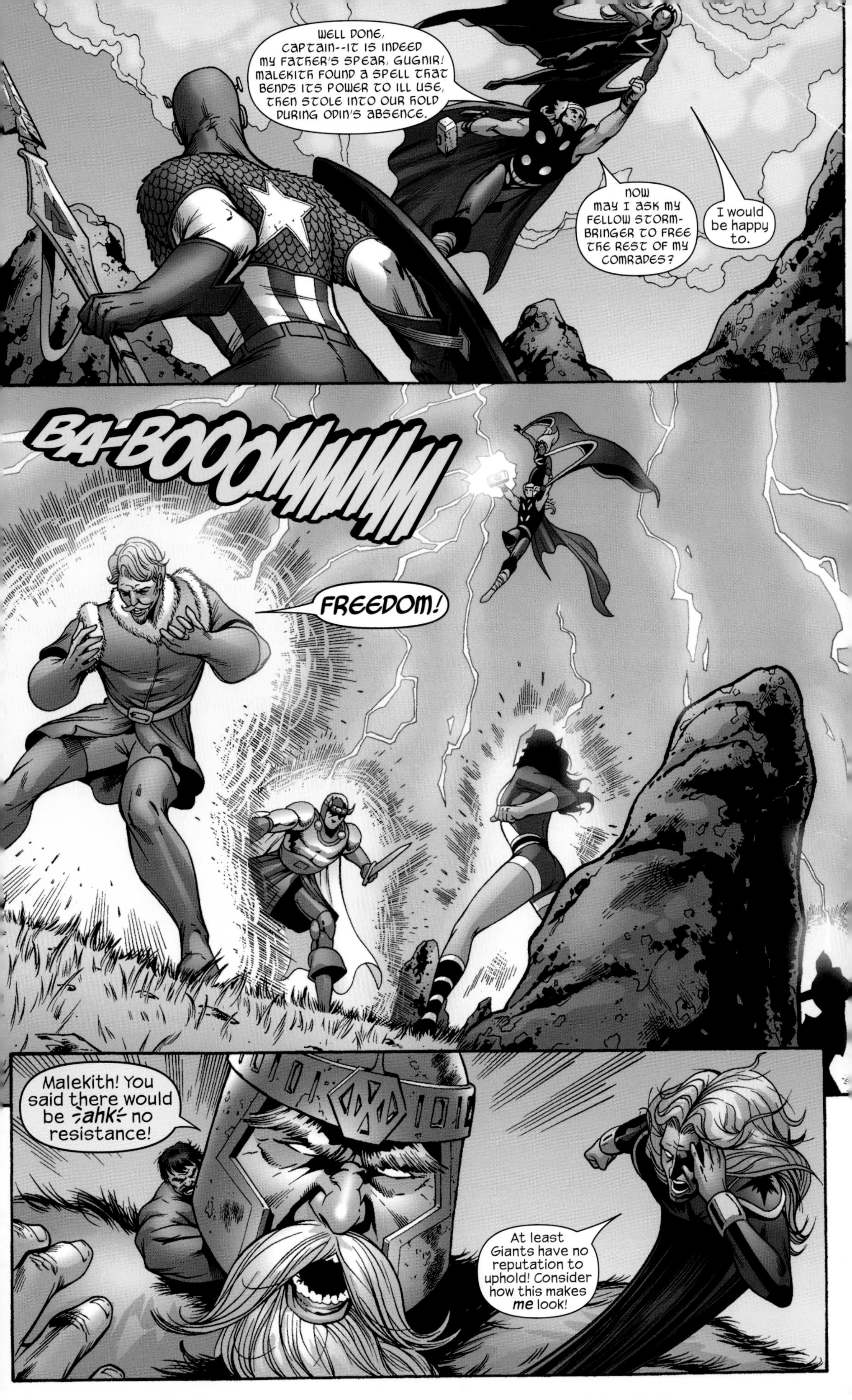
WELL DONE, CAPTAIN--IT IS INDEED MY FATHER'S SPEAR, GUGNIR! MALEKITH FOUND A SPELL THAT BENDS ITS POWER TO ILL USE, THEN STOLE INTO OUR HOLD DURING ODIN'S ABSENCE.
NOW MAY I ASK MY FELLOW STORM-BRINGER TO FREE THE REST OF MY COMRADES?
I would be happy to.
BA-BOOOMMMMM
FREEDOM!
Malekith! You said there would be ;ahk; no resistance!
At least Giants have no reputation to uphold! Consider how this makes *me* look!

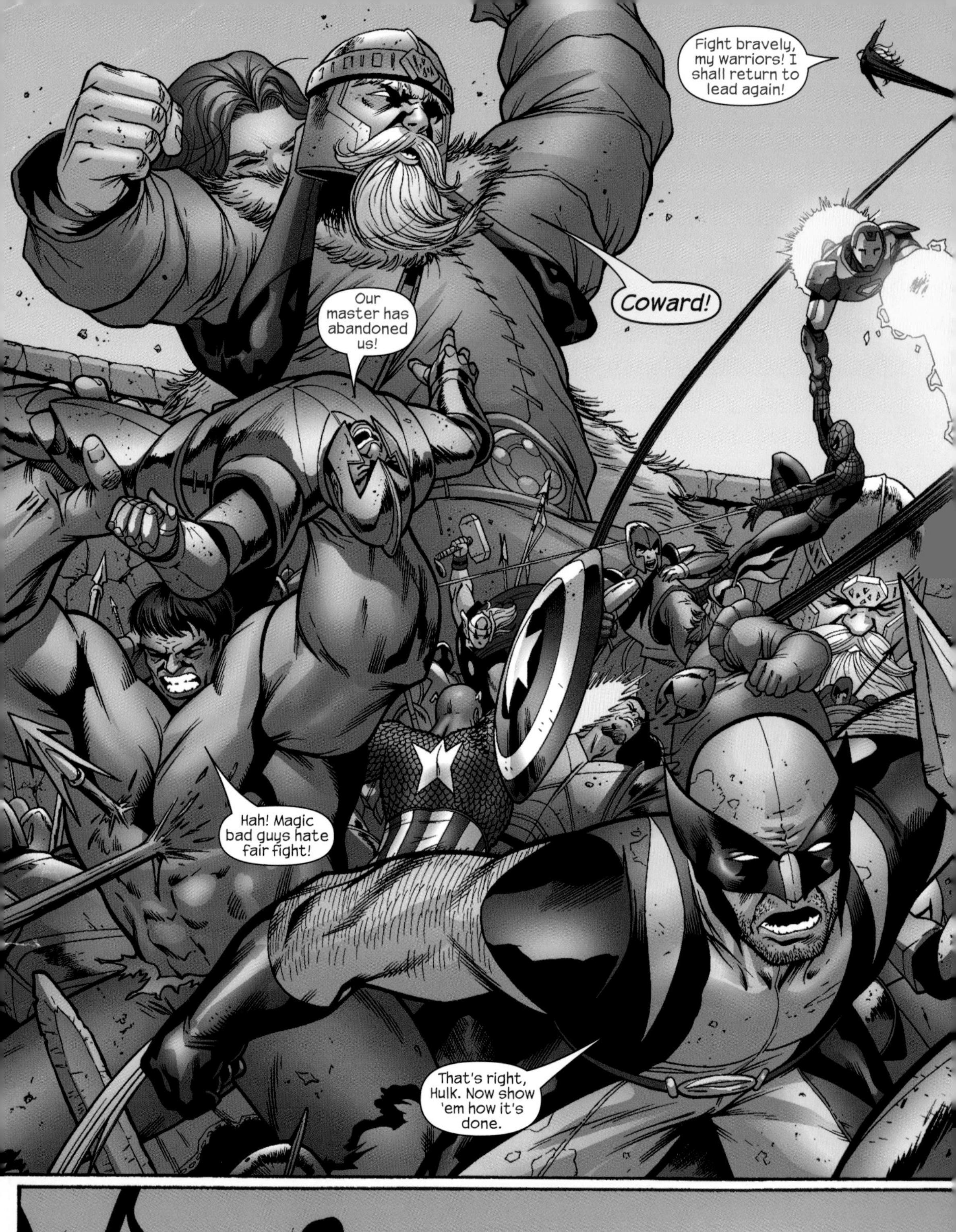
Fight bravely, my warriors! I shall return to lead again!
Coward!
Our master has abandoned us!
Hah! Magic bad guys hate fair fight!
That's right, Hulk. Now show 'em how it's done.

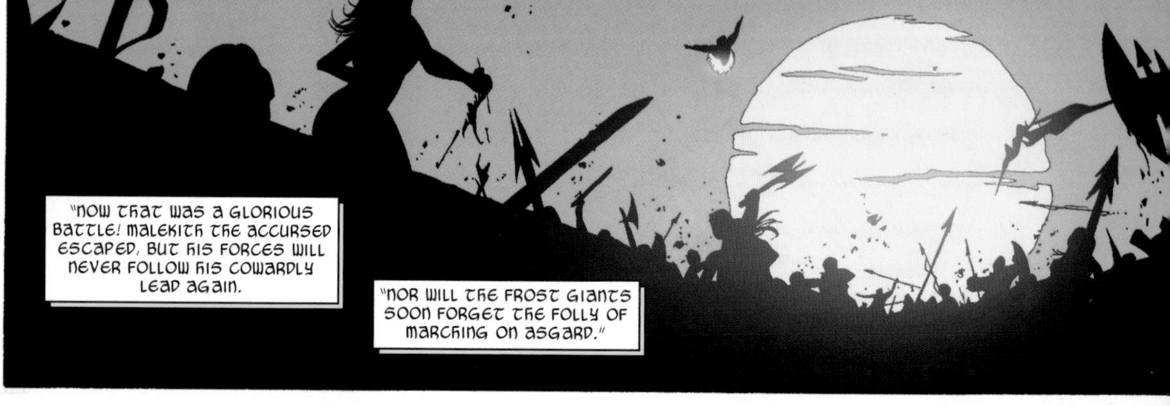
"NOW THAT WAS A GLORIOUS BATTLE! MALEKITH THE ACCURSED ESCAPED, BUT HIS FORCES WILL NEVER FOLLOW HIS COWARDLY LEAD AGAIN.
"NOR WILL THE FROST GIANTS SOON FORGET THE FOLLY OF MARCHING ON ASGARD."

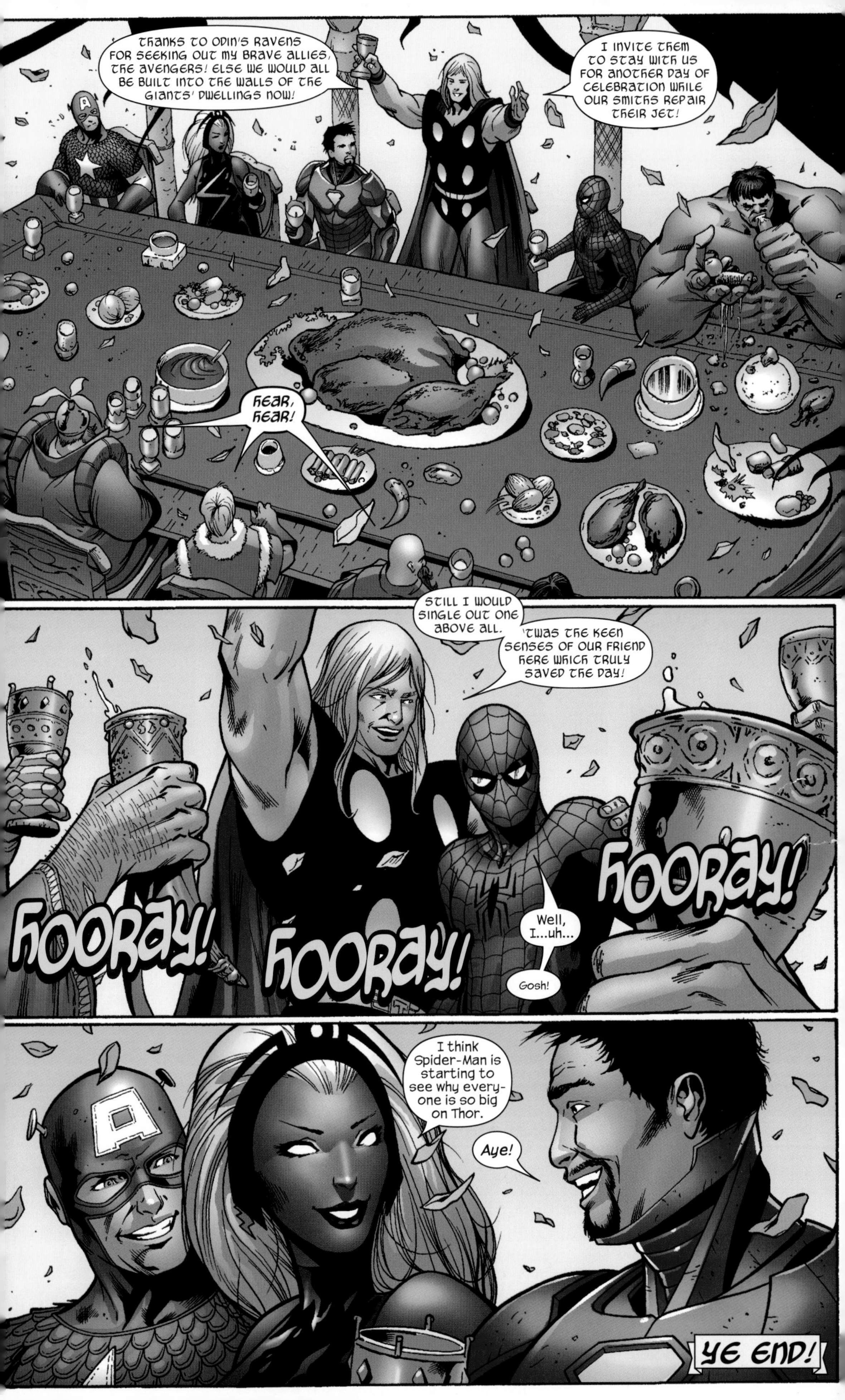
THANKS TO ODIN'S RAVENS FOR SEEKING OUT MY BRAVE ALLIES, THE AVENGERS! ELSE WE WOULD ALL BE BUILT INTO THE WALLS OF THE GIANTS' DWELLINGS NOW!
I INVITE THEM TO STAY WITH US FOR ANOTHER DAY OF CELEBRATION WHILE OUR SMITHS REPAIR THEIR JET!
HEAR, HEAR!
STILL I WOULD SINGLE OUT ONE ABOVE ALL.
'TWAS THE KEEN SENSES OF OUR FRIEND HERE WHICH TRULY SAVED THE DAY!
HOORAY!
HOORAY!
Well, I...uh...
Gosh!
HOORAY!
I think Spider-Man is starting to see why every-one is so big on Thor.
Aye!
YE END!

THE AVENGERS COLLECT THEM ALL!

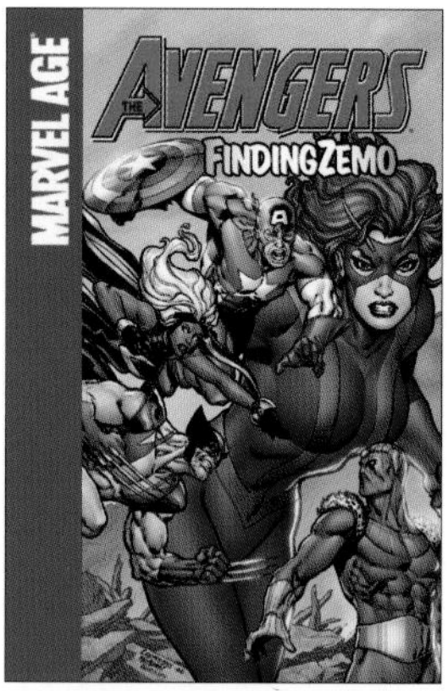
MARVEL AGE
THE AVENGERS
FINDING ZEMO

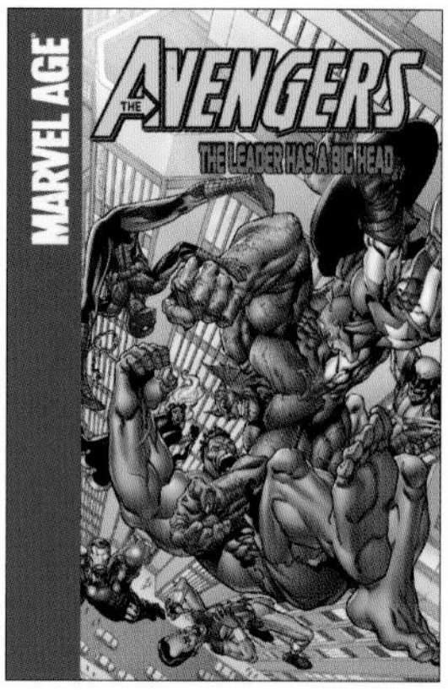
MARVEL AGE
THE AVENGERS
THE LEADER HAS A BIG HEAD

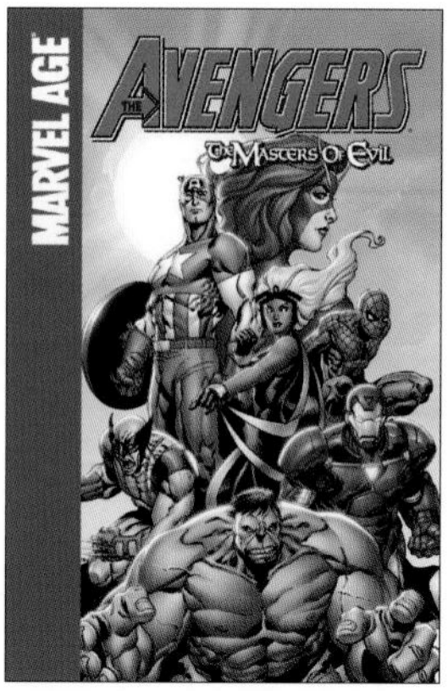
MARVEL AGE
THE AVENGERS
THE MASTERS OF EVIL

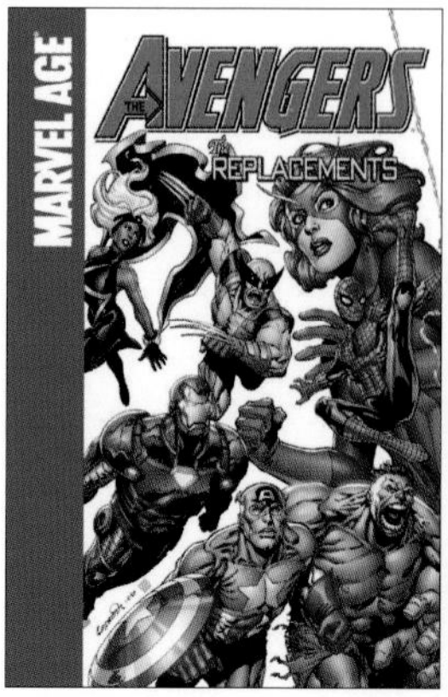
MARVEL AGE
THE AVENGERS
THE REPLACEMENTS

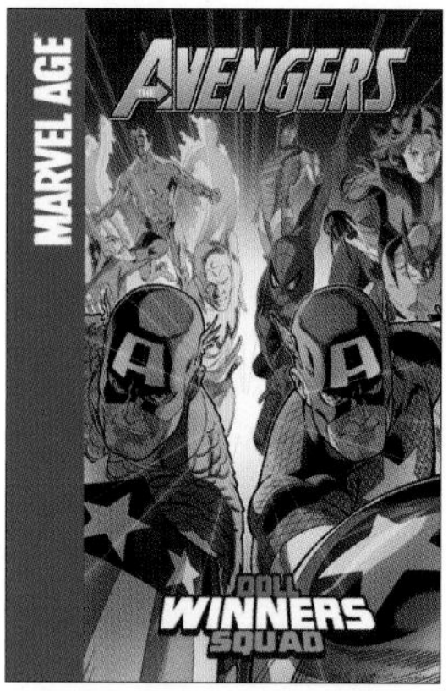
MARVEL AGE
THE AVENGERS
WINNERS
SQUAD

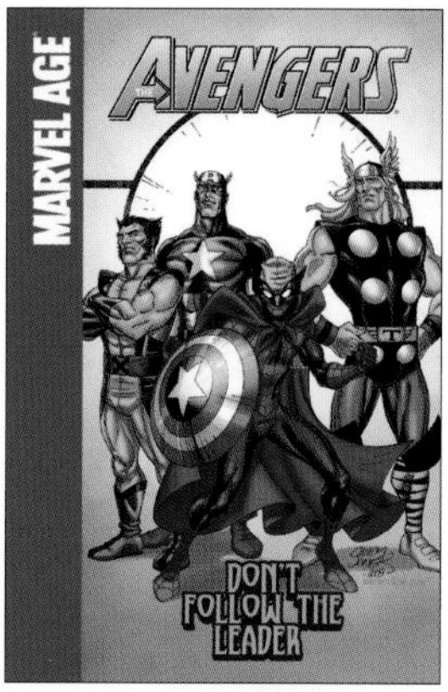
MARVEL AGE
THE AVENGERS
DON'T FOLLOW THE LEADER

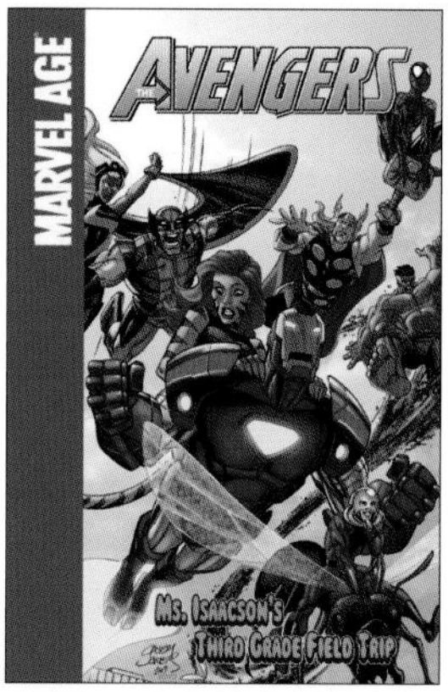
MARVEL AGE
THE AVENGERS
MS. ISAACSON'S THIRD GRADE FIELD TRIP

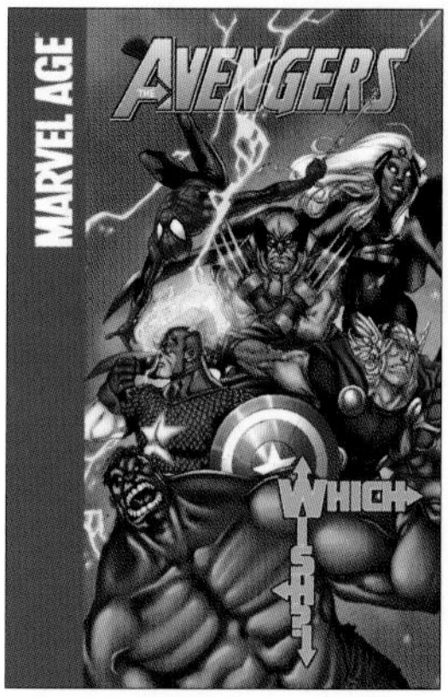
MARVEL AGE
THE AVENGERS
WHICH

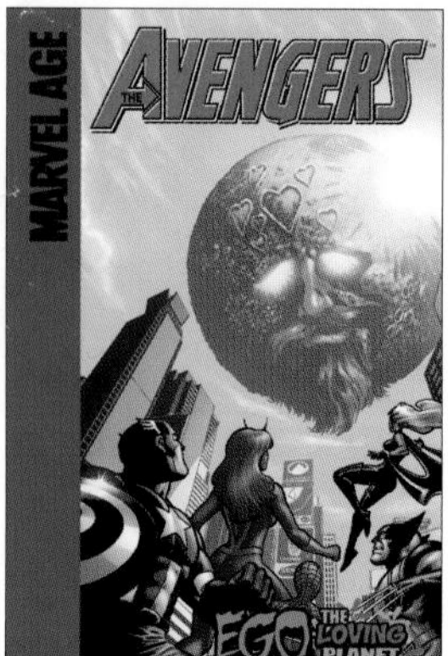
MARVEL AGE
THE AVENGERS
EGO THE LOVING PLANET

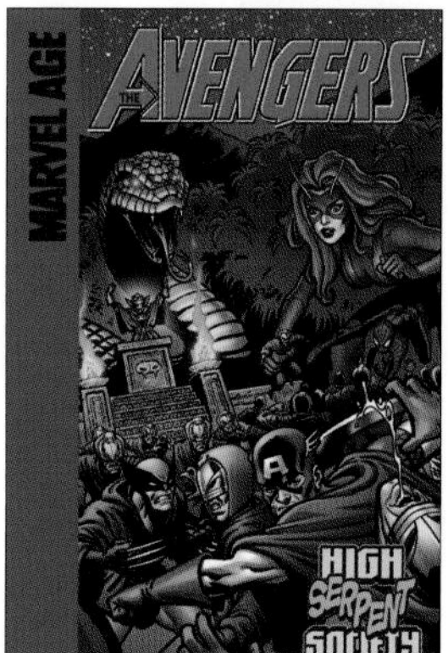
MARVEL AGE
THE AVENGERS
HIGH SERPENT SOCIETY

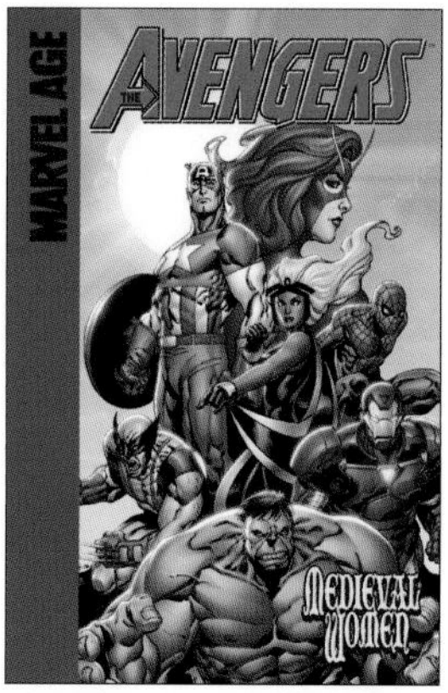
MARVEL AGE
THE AVENGERS
MEDIEVAL WOMEN

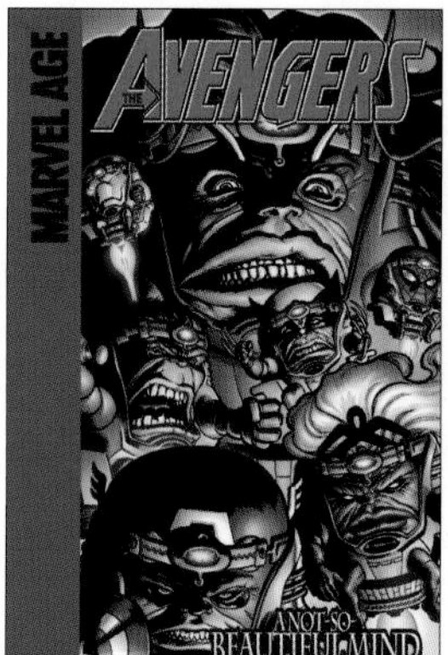
MARVEL AGE
THE AVENGERS
A NOT-SO-BEAUTIFUL MIND

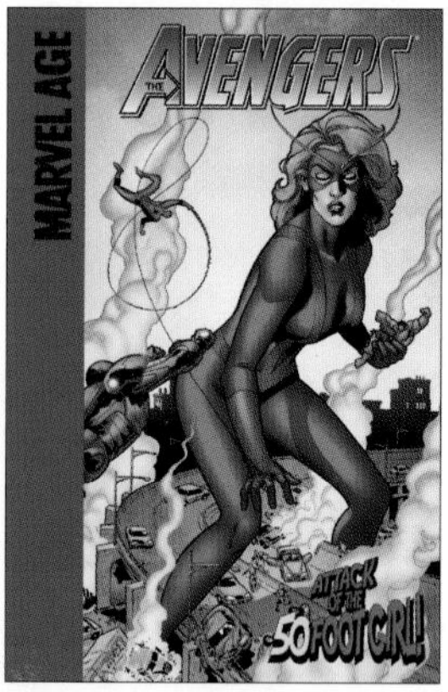
MARVEL AGE
THE AVENGERS
ATTACK OF THE 50-FOOT GIRL!

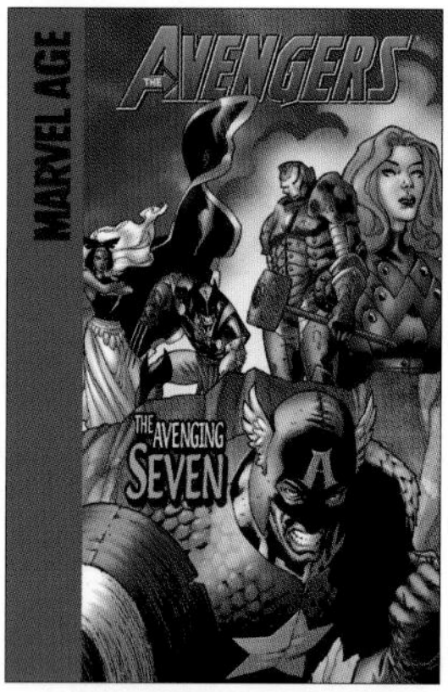
MARVEL AGE
THE AVENGERS
THE AVENGING SEVEN

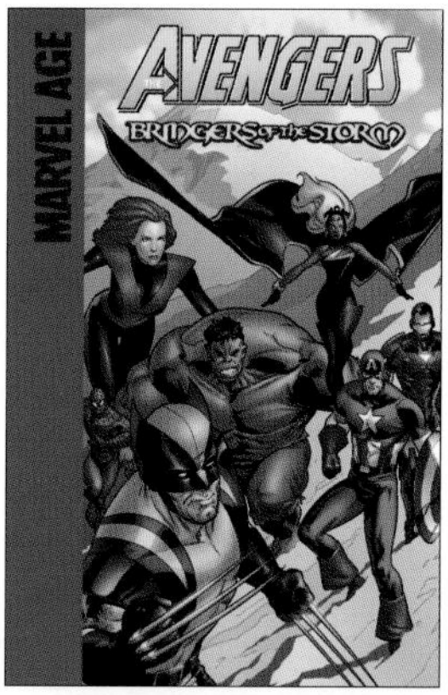
MARVEL AGE
THE AVENGERS
BRINGERS OF THE STORM

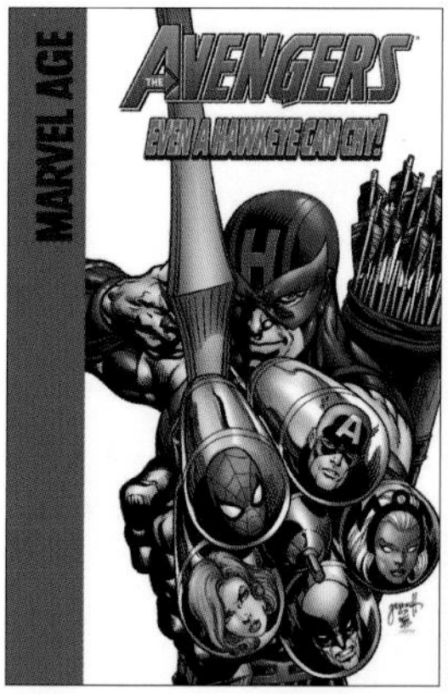
MARVEL AGE
THE AVENGERS
EVEN A HAWKEYE CAN CRY!

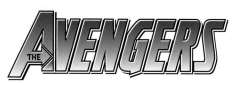